THE
NEVER
KING

VICIOUS LOST BOYS BOOK ONE

NIKKI ST. CROWE

BLACKWELL HOUSE

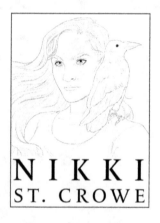

N I K K I
ST. CROWE

Copyright © 2022 Nikki St. Crowe
ISBN 13: 979-8-9854212-1-7
PUBLISHED BY BLACKWELL HOUSE LLC

To all the girls who had to grow up hard and fast.

BEFORE YOU READ

THE NEVER KING IS A REIMAGINING OF *PETER AND WENDY*, though all characters have been aged up and are 18 and over. This is not a children's book and the characters are not children.

Some of the content in this book may be triggering for some readers. If you'd like to learn more about CWs in my work, please visit my website here:

https://www.nikkistcrowe.com/content-warnings

"Feeling that Peter was on his way back, the Neverland had again woke into life."

- J. M. Barrie, Peter and Wendy

1

WINNIE DARLING

I haven't attended a normal high school in over two years, but yet I find myself still hooking up with the star quarterback in the passenger seat of his SUV.

He is bad at sex. Magnificent on the football field.

If only I liked football and hated sex.

Anthony shoves inside of me and I make the porn star face for him because I know he likes it.

I pretend to orgasm with him.

I am not a porn star, but I am the daughter of a prostitute so I think that's close enough.

"Oh fuck yeah, Winnie. Fuck. Oh baby." His grip on me is loose and clammy. He's trembling like the boy he is.

We're the same age, but decades apart.

"Fuck," he says and breathes hot air against my naked chest. "That was so good. Was that good?"

The lack of confidence is insufferable. I don't know that I've ever slept with a confident man.

Or maybe that's wrong.

Maybe they're only confident in the taking.

"So good, baby. You're so good at sex."

And I am so good at lying.

He smiles up at me as I continue to straddle him and then he stretches up and plants a kiss on my mouth.

I feel nothing other than a dull ache in my body and a throbbing headache behind my eyes.

I am dead inside.

And so fucking bored.

And the only thing I have to look forward to is being kidnapped by a myth.

Happy fucking birthday to me.

Anthony zips himself into his jeans and then drives me home.

I stare out the passenger side window as the SUV winds through my neighborhood.

When he pulls up to the curb, I start to open the door but he grabs my arm and leans over for a kiss.

I begrudgingly give it to him.

"You coming to the party this weekend?" he asks, more hopeful than I'd like.

When you're extremely giving with sex, you are always invited to the parties. So many parties. All of them the same. But I like familiar things. I've always been short on familiar.

"Text me," I tell him, because I'm not sure where I'll be this weekend.

Today is my 18th birthday and every Darling woman that has come before me has disappeared on this day.

Some are gone a day, others a week or a month.

But they always return broken, with varying degrees of sanity intact.

I don't want to go mad. I like who I am, for the most part.

When I come in the side door, Mom is suddenly in front of me. "Where have you been, Winnie? I thought he'd already taken you and—" Her attention wanders and then she races to the nearest window and tests its latch.

She's muttering to herself as she works.

Pirates and Lost Boys and fairies.

And him.

She won't speak his name when she's awake, but at night, when she dreams, sometimes she'll wake up screaming it.

Peter Pan.

Mom has been hospitalized seven times. They say she's schizophrenic just like grandma and great-grandma and all of the Darling women before her.

A legacy of madness that I stand to inherit.

"Winnie!" Mom rushes up to me, her bone-thin hands wrapping around my wrists. Her eyes are wide. "Winnie, what are you doing? Get in the room!" She shoves me down the hall.

"It's still daytime. And I'm hungry."

"I'll get you—when *he*—okay, listen." Her gaze goes faraway and she frowns at herself, her grip loosening and my stomach drops.

Please, for the love of all the gods, I don't want to end up like my mother.

"He's coming!" she screams at me.

"I know." I use my soothing voice on her. "I know he is, but you have the house battened down better than a bomb shelter. I don't think anyone could get in."

"Oh, Winnie." Her voice catches. "He can get in anywhere."

"If he can get in anywhere, then why lock the windows? Why stay in the room?"

She pushes me over the threshold, ignoring my logic.

The "special room" is a work of art fueled by terror. You can read the frenzy in the rough brush strokes that adorn the wall. Runic symbols, painted like graffiti with more etched into the casing around the door.

There has been a parade of so-called witches and shamans and voodoo priests that have come into our lives and through our houses selling my mom the secrets of protection from *him*.

We don't have the money for it, but we spent it just the same.

"I'll get you something to eat," Mom says. "What do you want?"

"It's okay. I can—"

"No! I'll get it. You stay in the room. Stay in the room, Winnie!"

She races back down the hall, her gauzy white dress billowing behind her, making her look like a specter. A few seconds later, pots and pans bang around our kitchen even though I'm absolutely positive we have nothing that can go in a pot.

This is the nineteenth house we've lived in.

I know the number of houses, but I can't remember most of them. And when your walls blur together, it's hard to ever feel like you're home.

Mom said she thought maybe she could lose him—Peter Pan—if she kept us moving. We travel light. I have two bags and one trunk that I inherited from my great-

great grandmother Wendy. It's smaller than it looks from the outside and about twice as heavy as it should be.

I can't seem to get rid of it.

It's about the only thing we own that holds any value, the only thing that feels real.

Our current house is an exhausted Victorian with crumbling plaster walls, worn and nicked hardwood floors, and lots of empty rooms. We don't even own a couch. Furniture is too hard to move.

I collapse on the inflatable bed shoved into the corner of my special room and stare up at the ceiling where the curling graffiti has been done in blood. That was the witch from Edinburgh, said only blood would do.

And it had to be mine.

Maybe we're all mad, in our own way.

Mom makes me a peanut butter and jelly sandwich and brings a glass of tap water.

She watches me eat it, jerking every time the house creaks.

"Tell me about him," I ask her as I peel the crust from the top of the sandwich and eat it like a length of spaghetti.

Mom winces. "I can't."

"Why not?"

She taps her index finger at her temple.

From what I've gathered, she thinks some kind of magic keeps her from talking about him in detail so I only get bits and pieces. She tells me the magic wanes on new moons, but we're halfway to a full moon.

It's the tide and the full moon that brings all of the

monsters out. The wolves and the fairies and the lost boys. That's what she said.

"What *can* you tell me?" I ask her.

Huddled in the corner of the room on her cot, knees drawn to her chest, she considers this for a few seconds. I imagine she was beautiful once, but I don't know her as anything other than crazy. Her hair is dark and coarse like mine, but it's started to thin because of all the medication she's on. Her skin is ruddy, her cheeks hollow.

There are layers of cracks in her fingernails and circles beneath her eyes. She doesn't work anymore. She's on disability, but it barely pays the bills. And the more isolated she is, I think the worse she gets.

"I remember the sand," she says and smiles.

"The sand?"

"It's an island."

"What is?"

"Where he'll take you."

"And you were there?"

She nods. "Neverland is beautiful in its own way." She wraps her arms around her legs and folds into herself. "All of it is magic, so much of it you can feel it on your skin, taste it on the tip of your tongue. Like honeysuckle and cloudberries." She lifts her head, eyes wide. "I do miss the cloudberries. He misses the magic."

"Who? Peter Pan?"

She nods. "He's losing his grip on the heart of the island and he thinks we can fix him."

"Why?" I tear off a corner of the sandwich and mush the bread between my fingers, flattening it into a pancake. Jelly squirts out the edge. I'm trying to prolong it, trick my belly into thinking it's getting a five-course meal.

Mom lays her cheek to her knees. "They broke their promise," she mutters. "They broke their promise to me."

"What promise?"

"I don't know how to stop him," Mom whispers, ignoring me. "I don't know if it's enough."

"It'll be okay," I assure her. "I'm not worried."

None of this is real.

Except for the madness.

That I am worried about.

Will it be like a light switch? One minute I'm sane, the next I'm not?

The thought of losing my mind terrifies me more than some boogeyman.

※

When Mom falls asleep, I slowly slip out of the room.

A storm has rolled in and lightning flashes through the window, lengthening the shadows of the old Victorian.

I go to the bathroom in the hall and stare at myself in the mirror.

I don't recognize myself. It's like looking at a stranger. Some days I worry that if I reach out for my reflection, there will be nothing there.

I'm starting to look like her.

Carved clean. Exhausted.

I don't want to be mad.

And I'm just so fucking *tired*.

My cardigan slips off the bone of my shoulder and I catch a glimpse of a puckered scar. One to match the runes drawn on the ceiling.

I pull the collar back up.

The medicine cabinet is missing half a door, so the left side is open revealing several rows of pill bottles.

Take your pick.

I don't want to be mad.

I reach out for a bottle of ibuprofen. I've taken so many over the years, I barely know relief from them anymore.

The floor creaks beyond the hall.

I snatch my hand back.

Lightning flashes through the house again and thunder chases it.

When the rumbling ends, I hear a door shut.

Mom.

I race down the hall and hurry into the room, but she's still on the cot sleeping soundly.

My heart rams into my throat.

Another board creaks.

Maybe someone broke in, thinking the house was abandoned? We can barely afford the rent, let alone the utilities for a house this size. We hardly use the lights.

Slowly, I shut the bedroom door behind me, and slide the lock closed. We don't have any weapons, nothing practical. We spent all of our money on useless magic.

Breath held, I grit my teeth together.

The doorknob turns.

I slowly back away from it.

Has it started already? Have I already lost my mind?

Thunder cracks through the sky.

The lock thunks open as if by magic and a boot pushes the door in.

The hinges squeak.

I look at Mom again. Was there more to her stories than I was willing to believe?

That can't be true.

Can it?

Mom lurches awake. "Baby, what's the time—"

"Shhhh." I hurry to her side and give her a shake.

But it's too late. The door is open and he fills up its void.

I can't fucking breathe.

There is the distinct sound of a lighter being clicked open, then the rough spin of the metal wheel. The flame catches, sending light over his face as he burns the end of a cigarette.

Silver rings on his fingers reflect the flame. Dark tattoos cover his hands. There are several strips of string and leather tied around his wrists. He's tall, broad shouldered, and wearing a long coat with a stiff collar that stands up around his sharp jaw. Even though his body is hidden beneath the coat, I can tell he's corded with muscle by the mere suggestion of it in his biceps.

When he pulls the cigarette away from his mouth, I can't help but trace the veins that snake over his knuckles with a quick sweep of my eyes.

He expels the smoke with a purposeful breath.

"Meredith," he says, "it's been too long."

Mom's breath catches beside me.

Is this really happening?

"You can't have her!" she yells.

"As if you could stop me."

My heart leaps to my throat.

"Please," Mom says.

He takes a long hit from the cigarette, the embers burning brightly. I hear the tobacco crackle as smoke curls around his face.

There's a fluttery feeling in my chest that instantly makes me feel guilty.

I suddenly feel more awake than I've felt in years.

I should not be feeling anything other than dread in this moment.

This is real. Mom was telling the truth.

"Please," Mom says again.

"There is no time for begging, Merry."

He takes his first step over the threshold. So much for that magic.

I gulp down a breath, trying to quell the rapid beat of my heart.

Somehow, in the blink of my eyes, he's crossed the last of the distance between us. He takes a fistful of my t-shirt dress and yanks me to my feet. "We can do this the easy way or the hard way, Darling. Which will it be?"

I gulp, trying to dislodge the lump suddenly growing in my throat.

He watches me do it, watches my tongue dart out and lick my lips.

The fluttery feeling sinks lower and the guilt festers and turns cold.

He is my mother's urban legend come to life and I don't know what to do with him now that he's here.

"You have three seconds to decide," he tells me.

There's no hint of exasperation on his face, but I sense it, nonetheless. Like he's had this conversation a million times before and is always disappointed with its destination.

Mom rises next to us and starts pummeling his grip on me, but he's quick, almost too quick to follow when he drops the cigarette and lashes out, grabbing her by the throat.

"No," he says easily. "Don't make this more difficult than it needs to be." He turns back to me. "Go on, Darling."

He gets in close to my face, white teeth gleaming in the moonlight. He's almost too beautiful, too dream-like.

Maybe I'm already mad.

And if I'm mad, none of it matters anyway.

"I'm waiting," he says.

"The easy way, obviously."

His brow lifts in amusement. "Obviously?"

"Why would I choose the hard way?"

Mom loses her fight and goes quiet.

"First lesson," he says. "There is no easy way." He turns to Mom. "I'll bring her back, Merry. You know they always come back."

Then he drops her, snaps his fingers, and everything goes dark.

2

PETER PAN

IT TAKES ME TWICE AS LONG TO GET BACK TO NEVERLAND AND THE
treehouse with a Darling thrown over my shoulder.

She's light as a feather. Her rib bones are sharp enough
to hurt.

This Darling is not well.

Perhaps her spiderweb cracks means she'll be easier to
break open.

It's not carrying her that makes the trip harder—it's the
shifting between two worlds and my waning magic.

I have so little left to spare.

This one has to be the one.

I don't know what happens if she isn't.

I am this island. It won't survive without me.

When I walk in through the open front doors of the
house, the Lost Boys are waiting.

I've lost count of how many there are now and I can
never remember half their names, but the ones who matter

will be waiting for me in the loft beneath the canopy of the Never Tree.

I take the Darling up the wide staircase, hand trailing along the carved banister to keep me upright. Wrought iron lanterns flicker from their scrolled hooks.

I am so fucking tired.

I come into the loft to find Vane at the bar, the twins at the hallway. Leaves are floating down from the branches of the Never Tree. It's growing thinner by the day.

The tree is dying.

Little pixie bugs glow bright yellow amongst the leaves that remain and whenever I see that glow, it reminds me of Tink and it makes me angry all over again.

"The room ready?" I ask the boys.

Kas nods, his eyes scanning the Darling, her arms hanging limply behind me.

The twins follow me down the hall and to the spare bedroom. Vane doesn't come. Vane is only interested in making Darlings cry.

There is a lantern lit on a table by the window and the window is open allowing the ocean breeze to steal in.

I set the Darling on the bed. The frame takes no notice.

Bash closes the metal cuff around her wrist, the one attached to a chain bolted into the wall.

I collapse into the wingback chair and pull the steel case of cigarettes from my pocket, lighting one with the flick of the lighter. The flame dances in the darkness. I inhale, the flame following the current, and the tobacco crackles as it burns.

When the smoke fills my lungs, I feel infinitesimally better.

"How was she?" Kas asks.

If any of us has a bleeding heart, it's Kas.

"More stubborn than I'd like."

Bash is leaning against the wall just inside the doorway and light from the hall outlines him in flickering gold. "What about Merry?"

The ocean air turns cold. I lay my head back against the chair. "As mad as we left her."

The cigarette burns to the end. I close my eyes as the sun reaches the horizon line.

The closer it gets, the further away the magic feels.

I am nothing in the daylight.

Nothing but ash.

"Watch her," I order as I get up and make my way for the door. "But don't touch."

"We know the rules," Bash says, a little annoyed to be told what to do. But Bash has always loved pretty things and this Darling is prettier than the rest.

"Don't fuck the Darlings," I say, just to be sure he hears me.

It's the only rule we have.

We don't fuck the Darlings because fucking Darlings is what got us into this mess.

We don't fuck the Darlings.

We just break them.

3

WINNIE

WHEN I WAKE, I HAVE THE SAME SENSATION I HAD WHEN I FELL asleep in the back of Mom's old car while she drove us six states west.

I'm not where I'm supposed to be, everything hurts, and nothing feels the same.

I hear the seagulls first.

We haven't lived near the ocean in seven years, but their squawk stirs the old memories of the sand coating our floors, the sound of the waves and the smell of the dune grass.

I've always loved the water. It makes me happy.

I hear an intake of breath after the gulls and the breath isn't mine.

When I open my eyes, I find a boy peering down at me.

No, not a boy exactly. He has the youth of a boy, but the presence of a man.

Long black hair is tied into a bun at the back of his head. His gaze is knife-like, sharp and glinting as he takes in the sight of me. His skin is the color of the bright side of a blood moon and black tattoos run over his bare chest. All of the lines are precise and symmetrical on both sides of his body. They start at his neck and travel like a labyrinth over the rest of him, disappearing beneath the waistband of ripped, black jeans.

He is a vision of dark virility.

"Good morning, Darling," he says.

"Where am I?" I lurch upright only to find I'm chained to a wall.

That's kinky.

"For your safety," he says, nodding at the chain.

"From what?"

"Wandering off." He smirks. He has full, puffy lips.

"She awake?" another voice says from the doorway.

I follow the sound and my brain stutters to a stop.

It's like I'm seeing double.

Except this guy's dark hair is cut much shorter and fans over his head in waves. The tattoos are exactly the same though, from what I can tell. This one is wearing a shirt.

"Before you ask," the new one says, "yes, you are hallu-cinating."

The other grunts. "Don't fuck with her, Bash. She'll get plenty of that later."

The one named Bash comes over. "How are you, Darling? Sometimes the journey here is hard on a girl."

My throat is raw and dry, my tongue like sandpaper in my mouth. I'm a little queasy and foggy, but other than that I seem okay.

Other than the fact I was kidnapped by someone I thought was a myth or a delusion and now I'm chained to a bed by the ocean. Back home, the closest ocean is several hundred miles away.

Just how far did they take me?

"I'm fine," I answer.

"Water?" the one by my bedside asks.

"Yes, please."

For my entire life, my mother prepared me for this moment, sometimes in the most painful of ways, and none of it was enough.

She literally told me this would happen and yet now that it is, it's still hard to wrap my head around.

Is it real? Or is this delusion how the madness begins?

The bed beneath me feels real. The warm tropical air, real. The space that the boys take up in the room, the energy that fills it—very, *very* real.

There is something about these boys that is more potent that any of the boys I've hung out with before and I've hung out with plenty.

Pretty boys always make the time go by faster. I hate being bored. But most of all, I hate being alone.

Bash disappears into another doorway on the other side of the room and returns with a cup of water. Condensation already blooms across the glass.

The gulls cry again.

I can hear waves crashing over rocks somewhere in the distance.

As I drink the water down—it's crisp and cool and somehow the most refreshing glass of water I've ever had—I take in my surroundings.

We're in a large room with crumbling plaster walls that look like they were once painted a bright shade of emerald. There are three rectangular windows to my right with slatted wooden shutters pulled open. There are no screens on the windows. Light pours in. Beyond, I can make out the branches of a palm tree and below it, a tree blooming with bright red flowers.

I'm on a bed with a thick wooden frame and what feels like a feather-stuffed mattress. The white sheet is clean, bleached to a crisp. There is no blanket.

A wingback chair sits in the corner with a long-armed lamp behind it and an end table.

That would be a nice place to sit to listen to the gulls if I wasn't chained to the bed.

I hand the glass back. The boy sets it on the floor. He must be sitting on a stool at my bedside because he's decidedly sitting but with no chair in sight.

"What am I doing here?"

The boys share a look and I swear I hear the distant chiming of bells.

Goddamn. I really am losing my mind.

"How much was your mother able to tell you?" Bash asks.

"Not much."

Last night was the first time she actually gave me any useful information.

My mother's boogeyman thinks I, a Darling, can fix him.

What can I possibly do for him? I can barely hold together my own life.

Bash leans against the wall behind his twin, a dark echo.

I went to school with twins once back when Mom and I lived in Minnesota.

The Wavey twins. The most obnoxious, annoying little girls I'd ever met. They used the fact that they were identical to get away with everything. Including putting worms in my peanut butter and jelly sandwich.

I wonder if these boys are the same.

They look like trouble. They feel like the wrong kind of temptation. Like a pretty tree frog that can kill you with a touch.

I think everyone has a super power, something they're just inherently good at and mine has always been reading people. Knowing what sort of a person someone is before they speak a word.

I think I need to be careful with these two if I'm going to survive this.

Whatever *this* is.

"I'm Kastian," the closest twin says. "You can call me Kas." He hitches his thumb over his broad, bare shoulder. "That's my twin, Sebastian."

"Bash," the other twin says.

"Hi," I say to them.

"We're the nice ones," Bash says and pushes away from the wall. He comes to sit at the end of the bed and the frame creaks beneath his weight. Even though he's fully clothed, I can tell by the way the material skims over his body that he's just as cut as his twin brother, all muscle and bone.

I've been alone in dark rooms with plenty of men, but none like the twins.

They could take me easily, in any way they wanted. Fighting them would be like fighting the ocean—pointless, futile.

But why would I?

They look like they'd be a wild ride.

I lick my lips and Bash's nostrils flare as his attention wanders to my mouth.

When you grow up around prostitutes, you learn a thing or two about tricks.

Mine has always been setting hooks.

"If you're the nice ones," I say, "then who are the mean ones?"

The twins share a look.

"Peter Pan?" I guess.

"Meaner than us," Kas admits.

"Not the meanest," Bash adds.

"Then who—"

Footsteps sound up the hallway beyond my room. The twins sigh almost in unison.

Bash scratches at the back of his neck. "Get ready, Darling."

"Why?"

My heart kicks up. There are more?

The footsteps draw closer, the heavy clip of a well-worn sole, the gait of someone who has a mission and will not be swayed from it.

Who is meaner than Pan? My mom never said anything about there being others. I never thought to ask.

When he darkens the doorway, the air gets lodged in my throat.

This one isn't as muscular as the twins, but there's something distinctly more sinister about him.

The scar. The eyes.

Three long, jagged scars cut his face in half diagonally from one temple to his jaw.

It's changed his gaze.

One eye is bright violet. The other pure black.

Goosebumps lift on my arms despite the warm air.

"The Darling is awake," the newcomer says in a cold, detached tone of voice. He comes over to Bash and steals the last of his cigarette, pinches it between his thumb and forefinger and takes a hit. When he speaks, he hasn't exhaled yet, so his voice is stilted as he holds the smoke in his lungs. "She started crying yet?"

Kas frowns. "Something tells me this one will be harder to break."

"They all break eventually," the mean one says, eyeing me with his unsettling eyes.

I automatically look away, my body singing with a creeping sense of dread. I draw back, try to make myself smaller.

Mom said there was magic here.

What kind of magic is this? I do not *shrink*. Not usually.

"Vane," Bash says. "Is that really necessary? She just woke up."

Sweat beads along my temple and there's a building terror threatening to spill out of my throat.

A scream builds in the base of my throat.

What is happening?

"Don't be a prick," Kas says.

The mean one—Vane—finishes the cigarette, narrowing his eyes at me as my heart drums loudly in my head.

My breathing quickens, hands clammy as I claw at the sheet. I can't sit still. I want to run. Tears blur my vision and then spill out.

"Vane," Bash says again with more force.

Like a tether cut, the terror is suddenly gone and I gasp out with relief.

"What the hell was that?" I pant.

"Darling," Kas says, and gestures to Vane with a flourish of his hand, "meet the scary one."

"What?" I'm still gasping for oxygen, tears streaming down my face. What the fuck?

"I told you they all cry eventually," Vane says. "Unchain

her. Bring her out. I can only take dumb Darlings for so long."

He disappears out the door.

"Come on," Kas says. "We'll fill you in while Bash makes you something to eat. Are you hungry?"

My stomach is queasy from whatever that just was, but it is decidedly empty too.

Maybe food will help.

Will anything help?

Mom warned me and I thought she was crazy and now I'm paying the price.

Kas is gentle as he removes the metal cuff. I see no key. I don't know how he unlatches it. The chain, with the cuff attached, is tossed to the bed.

The twins make their way to the door and wait for me at the threshold.

"We promise we won't bite," Kas says.

"Not yet, anyway," Bash adds.

4

BASH

How many Darlings have walked through the halls of the treehouse?

I've lost track.

We're on autopilot at this point, all of the steps rote, we've stepped so many times. I'll try to quell her with food. Kas will pretend he's not like the rest of us. Vane, of course, is about as subtle as a hammer and will terrorize her until she sobs.

It's a good thing I make damn good cloudberry pancakes.

The Darling's gaze wanders as we make our way to the kitchen. I'm distantly aware of the crumbling grandeur of the house. It's several hundred years old now, built by the labor of colonial soldiers we kidnapped back when it was easier to make men disappear.

They're dead now. Mortals decay. Lost Boys never die.

As we cross through the loft, the Darling gazes up in wonder at the canopy of the Never Tree.

When we built the house, we chopped the tree down, but the following day, it had resprouted, fully grown. Again we chopped it. Again it came back. So we built the house around it. Now it's home to wild parakeets and pixie bugs but it's looking worse than it ever has.

The leaves are thinning and the bark is peeling. It's just another sign that something is wrong with the island, and that something is Peter Pan.

When we reach the kitchen, Kas gestures to one of the stools at the long island in the center of the massive room. Mullioned windows take up one wall with a clear view of the ocean beyond. The kitchen has always been my favorite room. It's full of light and possibility.

The Darling sits.

Vane comes around the counter and looks menacing just by leaning.

As I collect the pan and bowls, the ingredients I need, I can't help but scrutinize the Darling.

We're all aware of the space she takes up.

Kas sits beside the girl. "What's your name, Darling?" His size dwarfs her. We could all break her.

"Like it fucking matters," Vane says.

Vane especially.

"Don't be a dick." To the Darling, Kas says, "For the most part, you can ignore him. He's always got a stick up his ass."

No, more like a ruthless shadow. But that's too much for the Darling yet. She'll learn soon enough.

"Go on," Kas says, keeping his tone of voice light.

"Winnie," she answers. "It's Winnie Darling."

"Nice to finally meet you, Winnie. You're Merry's daughter, right?"

She nods. There is an emotion that comes across her face at the mention of her mother. Defeat, I think.

Merry got a raw deal. We can all admit to that.

As I mix up ingredients, Kas entertains her with mundane conversation.

We all play our parts in this and my twin has always been the gentle tour guide. He's better at playing nice than the rest of us. He's more like our father in that way. I got our mother's thirst for blood.

I don't like to watch a Darling cry, but I love to watch them bleed.

In a bowl, I toss in the wet ingredients and stir it all together as Kas tells the Darling what she's won.

"We've been looking for something that was stolen from us," he says. "And we think you might be able to help us find it."

"What is it?" she asks.

That's what they all ask.

It's hard not to be bored with this conversation. How many more times can we have it?

Kas looks at Vane and Vane gives him a barely perceptible shake of his head.

It's always better if the Darling doesn't know the specifics. We don't want to muddle the memories in her head before we can dig our claws in.

"All you need to know," Kas says, "is that you're safe here so long as you follow the rules and cooperate."

"And for fuck's sake, don't run," Vane adds.

"Why?" she quips, a bit of fire in her voice.

Oh, I can see she and Vane are going to get along real well.

"Because I will chase you," he says, with a sinister bend

to his voice. "And you don't want to know what happens when I catch you."

The Darling visibly trembles.

Good girl.

The quicker she learns, the better off she'll be.

My twin eyes me. We've always been able to communicate on a level no one else can. We know each other better than we know ourselves sometimes.

His dark brow is furrowed.

He can feel it too.

Something is different about this one.

I know, I answer.

Pan has always had one rule about the Darlings—they're off-limits.

We have plenty on the island to keep us busy without fucking around with a Darling.

We're the Lost Boys and there's plenty of lost pussy looking to be found.

I'll make the pancakes and Kas will pretend to be the Darling's friend and Vane will brood from the corner and we'll try our hardest to keep it all together until sunset.

I quickly fry up a stack of three pancakes that I put on a plate for the Darling then cover it in a spread of butter, a layer of syrup.

Setting it in front of her, I stand back to watch her take the first bite.

"Dig in, Darling," I say. "I dare you to tell me they're horrible."

She looks at the food, then at me, as if she's trying to gauge whether or not I've done something to the food.

She's already been kidnapped. If we wanted her dead, she'd already be dead.

She cuts out a bite with the fork and when she puts it in her mouth, her eyes widen and a little moan escapes her.

My cock takes notice and I have to fight the urge to readjust.

Kas gives me a look.

I know, asshole, I say.

Pancakes aren't supposed to be fucking sexy. It's not like I gave her a bowl of strawberries to wrap her pretty little lips around.

I always make the Darling pancakes. It's tradition.

Down the length of the counter, Vane goes still.

She takes another bite and her eyes slip closed.

A bead of syrup glistens on her full lips and she drags the flat edge of her tongue over it, taking its sweetness.

Fucking hell.

Vane's shadow disturbs the air and when I look over at him, both of his eyes have gone black.

I snap my fingers at him. He blinks and turns away.

"It's really good," she says after swallowing. "Like... really, *really* good."

"Yes," I say. "I know."

Kas leans into her, spreads his arm over the back of her stool and steals the fork from her hand. I'm envious of his proximity to her.

What does she smell like? I ask him.

Like secrets and forbidden fruit.

Kas takes a bite off her plate. "Well done, brother," he says around a mouthful of food, then winks at me, the fucking prick.

"What's the tartness?" she asks.

"Cloudberries," Kas answers.

"Cloudberries are real?"

Her wonder is a delight.

Most Darlings have had a warning about us, about Neverland. Most of them show up terrified and trembling.

This one acts like she's awake for the first time.

"I like them," she says.

"They're in season," I say.

"Oh, she's here!" Cherry says from the doorway.

"Christ." Vane pushes away from the counter and makes his way to the door. I can't see his eyes. I don't know if he's gotten control of his shadow or not. Cherry is a good excuse for him to leave anyway. She's got the biggest crush on him, though only the gods know why. He's a fucking surly asshole on his best days. Downright scary on his worst.

He detests Cherry. He detests most of the women he fucks, but Cherry especially.

"She stinks like pirates," is his favorite thing to say.

Vane is gone in an instant and Cherry tracks him, desperate for his attention.

Somedays I feel sorry for the poor girl. But she made her choices. We all did.

"Morning, Cherry," I say. "Meet the new Darling."

Cherry comes up to the island and extends her hand to Winnie. "Hi! It's really nice to meet you!"

"Hi." The Darling sets down her fork, takes Cherry's hand and shakes. "Nice to meet you too."

"Are they being nice to you?" Cherry asks. "Sometimes they can be a little rough. Most Lost Boys are. They've been abandoned by their mothers and—"

"Cherry," I say, the warning clear. Kas and I may be the nice ones, but we won't hesitate to put her in her place.

"Sorry," she says. "I just mean..." Her face pinks. She's full of freckles, empty of confidence, lacking power. We might have mistreated her over the last two years. Actually, I know we did.

"You *mean* what?" The Darling looks between us. She's hunting monsters and has no fucking clue. Her gaze asks too many questions.

"Careful, Darling," I say. "Eat your food."

The sun is setting and Pan will wake soon.

And then the real fun will begin.

5

WINNIE

I can't remember the last time I had a meal cooked from scratch.

My mother has never been a cook and certainly never had the ambition to learn how.

One of my babysitters took me to a diner once and let me order pancakes and it was the first time I'd ever had them and when I told her that, she didn't believe me.

"How can you never have had pancakes?" she asked, forgetting that I had a mad mother and that if I needed something, I had to do it myself.

I devoured the entire plate of food and paid dearly for it that afternoon.

Bash's pancakes are fluffy in the center, crispy on the edges. The syrup is sweet and the cloudberries—I thought my mom was making them up, but they're so good. Like strawberries with a citrus tang to them.

I take another bite while the girl, Cherry, sits next to me. "Are there any pancakes left?" she asks.

"No," Bash answers.

Cherry's expression turns to immediate disappointment. She's freckled with auburn hair and big eyes that are a touch too close together. There's something about her that reminds me of a bubble on the verge of popping.

But I'm glad to see another woman here.

Mom only ever talked about Pan.

And she certainly never talked about the Lost Boys.

I don't think Cherry is a force to be reckoned with, but she's clearly desperate to be liked. I can use that to my advantage in a place like this.

"You can have some of mine." I slide my plate toward her.

"Really?" She looks like she doesn't believe me.

"Of course. I don't need them all."

"I beg to differ," Bash says. There's a hardness to his face now. "You're just skin and bones," he adds.

I swallow and tuck the folds of my sweater in around my body as if I can hide it and all of its imperfections.

He's not wrong. When you're poor and your mother is insane, your fridge is always lacking and your stomach always empty. You get used to it, though. The constant gnawing of hunger. Some days starving is the most real thing I feel.

"If I eat that entire plate," I tell him, "I'll be sick."

Kas gets up. "Can I talk to you for a minute?" he says to his twin.

Bash's gaze lingers on me before he finally leaves the room following in his brother's wake.

I woke up chained to a bed—are they not worried I'll try to run? Vane made it clear that it was a very bad idea.

But what comes after this?

What are they looking for?

"So," I say, turning to Cherry. She's devoured half the stack of pancakes and slows once my attention is on her. "Tell me what I need to know about this place. About those boys."

She winces. "I'm not supposed to talk about it."

"Why not?"

She swallows hard, bites her lip again. "It's...complicated."

"Did they take you too?" I ask.

"No." She shakes her head as if to prove the point. "I came of my own free will." There's pride in that statement.

"From where?"

"The other side of the island."

If she chose to come here, maybe they aren't as bad as I thought.

Maybe it's just Pan I have to worry about.

Well...and maybe Vane.

"Do you know what they're looking for?"

She slides the plate back to me. Her expression has sobered, the light dimming from her eyes. "The Lost Boys are older than they look. And Pan is much, *much* older. Older than me. Whatever happened, it was before my time."

"But what does that mean? *What* happened?"

The twins come back into the room. Bash snaps his fingers at Cherry and she quickly scurries away.

"Finish up, Darling," Kas says.

"Why?"

There's a double door on the far end of the kitchen with a balcony beyond it and the ocean beyond that. Bash goes to it and looks out.

The sun is setting. There are no clocks here so I have no idea what time it is. Sunset at home is around eight p.m.

but for some reason, it feels later here. Maybe it's the tropical air.

"Because Pan will be up soon," Bash says to the door. "And he'll want to see you."

A shiver rolls down my spine.

I get a flash of the myth in my mind, the dark stranger that came to my house last night and stole me away, just like my mom said he would.

The guilt comes back. I never believed her.

I should have.

6

PETER PAN

Beyond my tomb, I can feel the sun sinking toward the horizon line, the shadows growing long.

But it's dark in here.

And when you wake to total darkness, it's impossible not to feel buried.

Some nights I wake and wonder if I'm in hell.

If I'm already fucking dead, entombed in the island's dirt.

I toss the sheets back and set my feet to the stone floor and it's the chill that brings me back, tells me that I'm still in my body.

I have flesh and bones, but still no fucking shadow.

How much longer?

How much longer do I have?

I flick on the bedside lamp and golden light fills the room. Immediately my eyes burn.

Fuck, I feel like hell.

I find my pants in the corner, the belt still strung through the loops. I pull them on, toss on a shirt and roll up the sleeves.

My sword is where it always is, hanging on the hook by my bed.

When the sun can kill you and pirates are hunting you and your magic is fucking waning, all you have left are blades.

I leave off the sword but go heavy on the knives.

One each goes in my boot. A few more hidden beneath my pant legs. Another in a sheath on my forearm.

Two floors above me, I hear Bash tell the Darling to sit.

She sits.

If she's a good girl, she'll always do what we tell her.

And I can be rather convincing.

The lock on my outer door clanks open. Vane's the only one with a key. His footsteps draw near. He doesn't bother knocking because Vane is a self-entitled prick like that.

Of course, he has his shadow. He has his magic and all of the perks that come with it.

"Good," he says when he comes in. "You're up."

I sit back down on the edge of the bed and run my hands through my hair. I need a drink.

"You don't look well," he adds.

I glance up at him. He's leaning against my dresser looking like he was carved from war.

I'm still not sure how I convinced him to join me and the Lost Boys but I'm glad I did. I need him by my side. Now more than ever.

"That trip took a lot out of me," I admit.

"I told you I'd go fetch her."

I snort. "And have her come back in two pieces?"

He runs his tongue along the inside of his bottom lip but doesn't argue with me.

I get up as the last drop of sunlight disappears. I can feel it in my veins. Like a tether untied.

I can finally breathe.

"How is she?" I ask.

Vane's gaze darkens. "Prettier than the last."

"Not what I asked."

He sighs. "Bash made her pancakes. Kas was nice to her. She's calm for now. Already asking too many questions. Cherry gave her too many answers."

"Fucking Cherry."

"She's a liability. Why the fuck do we keep her around?"

"Because she's collateral and the kind of loyal we need. That's why."

"She *was* loyal when the twins were fucking her. Now she's desperate."

"She's desperate for you," I remind him and disappear into the bathroom. "The twins were just a distraction. She wants you. So fuck her and keep her loyal."

I can hear him grumbling in the other room.

At the sink, I splash cold water on my face, try to drive the ache from my muscles.

I am ancient.

I shouldn't ache.

I'm running out of time.

I can feel the island slipping from my grip.

In the mirror, I don't recognize my reflection. I am a king who has no throne.

Fucking Darlings. Fucking Tink.

The rage simmers in my gut. I grit my teeth, close my eyes, summon a breath.

This one will be the one.

She fucking has to be.

Hands still damp, I rake my fingers through my hair. The cool water feels good on my scalp, helps soothe some of the pounding behind my eyes.

Out in the room, Vane is still brooding.

"What?" I say. "Spit it out."

"Just let me kill Cherry. Let me send a message."

"No."

"Pan."

"When's the last time you chased someone, anyway? I can feel your shadow simmering. You got energy that needs to be spent. Do it before you take it out on the Darling. Do it for me."

He sighs again. "Fine. Fuck."

I give him a hard pat on the back. "Now let's go get a drink."

Our footsteps echo in the underground tower as we wind up the wrought iron stairwell. When we emerge on the main floor of the treehouse, I take in a deep breath of the salty sea air.

In the distance, gulls cry as they fight over scraps.

I can't see the Darling yet, but I can feel her.

We are a house of cold, hard edges.

She's already made it feel warmer and I've barely known soft or warm in my life.

The Lost Boys like to joke that I ran away from my mother the moment I was born.

But if I am honest about it, I think the island birthed

me. I have no memories before I woke up here shrouded in magic.

Down the hall, Kas laughs at something and Bash snorts.

I smell rum on the air, which means the twins are already drinking. Little fuckers are the little brothers I never wanted or needed.

Vane and I go up the grand staircase and come in on the loft. Some of the wild parakeets are perched on the branches of the Never Tree, their soft warbles indicating they're falling asleep.

I miss the sound of their chirping.

I miss a lot of things about the daylight.

When I step through the doorway, the Darling's eyes track me.

She can't help it.

No one can.

Even a king without a throne demands attention.

"He has risen," Bash says.

I glare at him as I go to the bar. We have hundreds of bottles of liquor that are lined up on the shelf in front of a wall of mirrors patinaed with age and cracked by care-lessness.

As I reach for my favorite bottle, I look up in the mirror and catch the Darling staring at me in the reflection.

Blood rushes to her cheeks and she quickly looks away.

I pour a shot of rum then add a few ice cubes to the glass and finally turn to the room, to her.

She still won't look at me.

I take a swig, let the alcohol roll around on my tongue before swallowing it back, let the burn settle in. It reminds me that I'm alive.

Aren't I?

I snap my fingers at Bash and he brings me the steel cigarette case, flips it open for me so I can pluck one out. I pull the lighter from my pants pocket, flick the wheel and light the end of the cigarette.

The smoke burns differently than the liquor, but it burns just the same.

I am alive.

I am alive.

The Darling sits on the leather sectional in the very center. The large couch makes her look small. Her bones are sharp against her sweater.

She'll pay a cost for a debt she knows nothing about.

I do feel sorry for her, the little Darling girl. But not sorry enough.

I take a hit from the cigarette, let the smoke leak out before sucking it back in with a deep inhale.

This catches her eye.

She swallows hard, then zeros in on the blade strapped to my arm.

I can hear the rapid beat of her heart, but I don't think she's scared so much as intrigued. Time to teach her the first lesson.

"Get up," I tell her.

She looks to Kas.

"He can't help you," I say. "Get up, Darling."

She rises. She has no shoes on and the bones of her feet stick out from her flesh like the spines of a lion fish.

What did Merry do to her?

The rage comes back, but this time it's kindled by something else.

Something I don't like.

"Vane," I say and he falls in step beside me. "Darling. Follow us."

"Don't run," Bash warns her. His tone is light, but the warning is serious. If she knows what's good for her, she'll heed it.

We go out through the bank of doors that leads to the balcony where stairs wind down to the patio. There's a fire burning in the stone pit and Lost Boys hanging around, drinking and cavorting with some of the girls from town. One of them is quietly strumming on a guitar.

When they see us coming, the guitar lets out a twang, then goes quiet as they all rise and bow their heads as we pass.

The Darling's pace falters.

"Keep up," Vane warns her and gives her a shove.

She walks.

I take one last hit from the cigarette, then flick it into a nearby pot. It's full of rainwater from yesterday's storm and the ember sizzles.

The patio breaks to hard packed earth where a root-covered path winds through the palm trees and large auris plants. Firecracker flowers and bright hibiscus blooms hang over the path.

The Darling plucks a firecracker from its stem and rolls the petals between her fingers, then smells the oils left behind.

Down the hill, the ocean laps against the shoreline. The gulls have caught a headwind and are hovering in flight, their wings tipped in the silver light of the nearly full moon.

That's another thing I miss—flying.

We go down to the beach, the white sand squeaking beneath our steps.

The wind is coming out of the north and I swear I can smell the filth of pirates.

"Look around you, Darling," I say.

She's caught between me and Vane, her arms folded over her chest.

She looks down the shoreline, south, then north. My territory is the entire south end of the island, from the point of Silver Cove to the craggy outline of Marooner's Rock. Hook's territory is on the other side, on the north end of the island, with Tilly's territory like a pie wedge between us.

"This is Neverland," I tell the Darling. "This place does not exist in your world."

She takes in a breath, her shoulders rising before quickly deflating again.

"You can swim for miles in any direction and you'll get nowhere, especially not home."

The gulls cry out again, then turn into the wind and head south. The waves pick up as the tide rises.

"There is no escape. Do you understand what I'm telling you?"

She drags her tongue over her lips.

Vane goes rigid beside me.

"What am I doing here?" she asks and takes a step forward. "Why do you take the Darlings?"

She's rail thin, but full of fire.

"How long before I can go home?"

"Is that what you want?" I ask her. "To go home?"

"Why wouldn't I?"

"Answer the question."

"I don't want to be held captive." Her voice is rising and Vane's patience is thinning. "I can't help you with whatever it is you want," she says and drops her arms at her sides, hands curling into fists. "So you're wasting your time and... my mother...she needs me."

"Does she?"

"Yes!"

"This one is going to be a handful," Vane says, his voice rumbling in the back of his throat.

"I can't help you, so take me home and—" She cuts herself off, her eyes going wide.

The sharp bite of sulfur blooms on my tongue.

"Vane," I say.

The Darling backpedals, her heart rate spiking.

"Vane!"

She turns around and runs.

I grab Vane by the shoulders and give him a shake. Both his eyes are black and the blackness of the shadow is filling his veins, surging around his eyes like a writhing mask.

"You didn't tell me it was this bad."

He growls and yanks out of my grip. "I'm fine."

"You're not fine."

His attention zeroes in on the running Darling. Her feet pound at the sand, her sweater flapping behind her.

"Now I have to go chase her," I say. "Well done."

"No need. I'll chase her."

I grab him again before he gets away from me and yank him close. "If you catch her, there won't be anything left. And she is our last fucking chance."

The shade has turned his black hair white, turned his incisors to fangs.

Vane has never had a handle on his shadow, no matter how much he tries to convince himself, and me, otherwise. He's got his own demons to hunt.

"Go on," I tell him again.

He grits his teeth, lets out a long, disappointed growl.

He watches her another second before turning away and as he walks back up the beach, his hair fades to black again.

I'm running out of time, but I think Vane is too.

For fuck's sake. I don't have the patience for this.

The Darling is halfway down the beach now, the moonlight painting her in strokes of silver and blue.

I might not be able to fly, but I can still run, and the Darling never stood a chance.

7

WINNIE

I CAN'T BREATHE. I WASN'T MADE TO RUN.

The sand is uneven beneath my feet and it's making every step twice as hard as it should be. Tears are streaming down my face.

I hate fucking crying.

I don't cry.

How far do I run?

Why am I running?

Haven't they warned me over and over not to run?

The panic returns and this time, I think it's all me. This might be a tight situation I can't negotiate my way out of.

There's a cliff in the distance rimmed in the glow of the moonlight. Mist from the ocean waves glitters in the devouring night air.

Suddenly Peter Pan is in front of me and the terror steals the air from my lungs.

I lurch to a stop before I slam into him. He catches me easily, his grip rough on my arms.

"What the fuck did I tell you, Darling?" His voice is edged in rage.

"I don't know...I was..." I can't catch my breath. I don't know what is happening. "I was afraid," I admit, even though I don't remember *becoming* afraid.

Suddenly I just *was*, just like when I first woke up in the house and Vane came into the room.

For a split second, Pan softens.

I can sense it in the fading of the tension in his body. "That was Vane," he says. "He has the ability to make people feel terror.

"He...*what*?"

"If it's any consolation, he didn't mean it."

I laugh and for a split second, I hear my mother in my voice. The madness bleeding through.

"It's not," I say, "a consolation." I swipe at a tear as it trails down my cheek. "Is it like...magic or something?"

"*Or something*. Come on." He gestures back toward the house.

"I want to go home."

"Why?"

"Because...because you all are assholes."

"And?"

"And...and I don't want to be *broken*."

Raw emotion leaks through my voice. I didn't mean to show it but it came out anyway and now I can't take it back.

Pan frowns at me. "How much you break is entirely up to you," he says. "The more you fight it, the harder it'll be."

I snort. "Right. There is no easy way. I remember."

He reaches out for me again. I dance away.

"Darling," he says. "I'll throw you over my shoulder and carry you back if I have to."

"When do I get to go home?"

"As soon as I find out whether or not you can help me."

The wind picks up and the waves crash against the shore so I have to shout at Pan to make sure he can hear me. "And when is that?"

"Do you always ask so many fucking questions?"

"When I'm kidnapped, yes!"

"Christ." He runs his hand through his hair and turns away. "I'm beginning to think this is a curse."

"Just tell me—"

"No." He comes at me, grabs my arm, puts his shoulder to my chest and lifts me over his shoulder.

"Hey!"

"Fight me and I'll tie you up and drag you back to the house."

His arm is tight across the back of my thighs. I'm still wearing my t-shirt dress and the hem rides up. At any second, I could be flashing him.

But fighting him will only make the skirt ride higher.

I go limp against him, hanging over his shoulder and down the broad length of his back as he makes his way up the beach.

"Run again, Darling," he says, "and next time I'll let Vane chase you."

My heart thuds loudly in my ears. It felt like I might choke on the terror. I can't imagine what it must feel like to be chased by Vane while his...*magic*...does what it does.

Am I really going to believe in all of this?

Peter Pan came on my 18th birthday just like my mother warned me he would.

He came and he took me away.

I can't deny the reality of it any longer. The sooner I accept it all, the quicker I can figure out how to escape it.

Pan carts me back to the house and through the crowd of boys gathered around the bonfire. I can feel them all watching me, tossed over Pan's shoulder like a conquest.

Pan doesn't say anything to them and the guitar music picks up once we're on the stone balcony of the house.

Inside, I'm tossed unceremoniously on the couch with my skirt bunched around my waist.

The twins notice.

I take my time fixing it.

Pan goes to the bar and pours himself another drink. When he returns with it in hand, he sits in one of the plush leather chairs across from me. If the leather is anything like the couch, it's buttery soft to the touch.

Their house isn't ostentatious, but there are some things that speak to wealth. Like the furniture, the bar, all that liquor lined up like trophies.

Some of the house is crumbling with age, but there's beauty in it, like a cracked marble statue of some ancient Greek goddess.

Pan rests his tumbler of liquor on the arm of the chair and lays his head against the back and closes his eyes.

The twins give me a look that very clearly says, *What have you done?*

It was Vane. Not me. I'm pretty sure I wouldn't have run if he hadn't turned that power on me.

Bash pulls out another cigarette and lights it, takes a drag. Then he gets up and crosses the room and hands it to Pan.

Pan opens his eyes and takes the offering, pinches the cigarette between his thumb and forefinger as he takes a pull from it.

When he exhales, the smoke clouds above us and ghosts to the exposed beams.

To my left, the tree that has sprouted right up the center of their house lets a few more leaves loose and they flutter like feathers to the ground.

"Here's what you need to know, Darling," Pan says, but he's still looking at the ceiling, his head lolled back against the chair. "The Darlings took something from me a very long time ago and they hid it and I want it back. You're going to help me find it."

"I don't know where—"

"Quiet." His gaze lands on me. Now in the light of the house, I realize he has eyes so blue they're almost white and they are ringed in a circle of black.

A shiver dances across my shoulders and I tug my sweater closed.

"I don't need your permission to root around inside your head and I'm not asking for it." He sits forward. "But cooperate and we'll all get what we want much sooner than if you don't."

He takes another hit and smoke ribbons around his face.

I think this is the first time I've really looked at him. When he showed up at my house, I was too deep in the disbelief to really take him in.

On the beach, he was shrouded in darkness.

The sleeves of his shirt are rolled up to his elbows, exposing black ink that covers both his arms and hands. The silver rings on his fingers glint beneath the light as he holds his glass in a death grip.

The tattoos are distracting and I'm grateful for it. It's difficult to look him straight in the face.

When I look at him, my belly soars.

There is something about him that is disarming. Unnatural. *Haunting*. Like a barren tree growing in the middle of a dark lake.

Something that very rarely should be and yet is.

Just the sight of it tells you a story—I am indestructible. Unyielding.

It's hard to look at him, but harder to look away.

"Do you understand me, Darling?" he says.

I swallow around a lump wedged in my throat. "Yes."

"Good girl." He gets up. "Put her back in her room."

The twins share a look.

"Now."

They move as Pan disappears from sight.

"Come on, Darling." Kas pulls me upright as Bash starts down the hall. "We'll tuck you in and we promise we'll be nicer than Pan." He ends this with a laugh that feels like it could be sarcastic.

They lead me down the hall to the back bedroom and chain me to the bed again. Kas is gentle, but I catch his gaze lingering on my body.

It's an odd feeling, suddenly being held captive in a house full of boys.

A year ago, I'd call this a party.

Now it's just the sum of a life lived in fear and delusion.

"For your first day in Neverland," Bash says, "you did all right, Darling."

"I'm chained to a bed. It isn't like I had a choice in any of this."

Kas's jaw flexes. "We always have a choice."

"If you need us, we'll be within shouting distance, Darling," Bash says and then they leave me in the flickering light of a lantern, the door clicking closed behind them.

8

WINNIE

I SPENT THE SUMMER OF MY THIRTEENTH YEAR LIVING WITH MOM in a rundown house that was crammed between two warring neighbors, one a prude and the other a prostitute.

Starla was the prostitute, an acquaintance of Mom's who helped us get the rental.

Beth Anne was the prude and she hated Starla. "That vile woman," she used to say when she looked down the stretch of cracked sidewalk to Starla's cute yellow cottage. "She's a blight on this neighborhood."

The most ironic part about that was that Starla's house was easily the nicest on the block.

It didn't take me long to realize that Starla was rich and her body her currency and she knew better than Mom how to use it.

Beth Anne was secretly envious of Starla, as much as she pretended otherwise.

I don't think it was the freewheeling sex so much as it was the freedom.

Beth Anne's husband ignored her and probably hated her. She was trapped and she hated that Starla wasn't.

I loved Starla. I loved listening to her and watching her and learning from her.

"I want to be a millionaire," she told me one afternoon while she babysat me for Mom. "I'm close. Just a few more years and I'll be worth seven figures."

The money was hard to imagine, but really, it was Starla's confidence that I couldn't wrap my head around.

How did she do it?

How did she exist in her skin and love being there?

I studied her that entire summer, tried to learn her secrets. I'd always loved watching people. I found they were much easier to read when they didn't realize they were being watched.

Starla was always quick to start a conversation with people and she had a habit of touching them, even complete strangers. A hand on the shoulder, a squeeze of an arm. Men loved this. And it didn't matter where we were or what Starla was asking, the men would bend.

One afternoon she somehow talked a man, a stranger, into buying us lunch. At the end of the summer, she pulled into her driveway in a brand-new SUV that some guy bought her off the lot.

"Is he your boyfriend?" I asked her.

She laughed. "Baby girl, I don't do boyfriends. Men are my toys and I play with them regularly."

I wanted her to be my mother.

When we lost that rental house because Mom got behind on the rent, I was devastated. Starla told me I could come visit her whenever I wanted, but Mom could only find an apartment two counties away.

I never saw Starla again.

Sometimes I think about her and wonder whether or not she made it to seven figures.

I'm sure she did.

As I lay chained to a bed in a place I don't recognize, I can't help but ask myself what Starla would do.

She wouldn't be worried. She wouldn't be afraid. Starla would come up with a plan and she'd take action.

Before Pan, before Neverland, I thought my fate was to go mad just like my mother and that nothing could stop it from happening. I thought crazy was in my blood but now I think it happens here. In Neverland.

So I need to figure out how to stop it from happening. And the fact that I have the opportunity to stop it is more than I ever thought I'd get.

I'd never been a prude, not like Beth Anne. I didn't have the luxury of it.

It was why I went through half the basketball team freshman year of high school. They all gave me things I wanted and needed. Sometimes a ride to school. Sometimes food. Other times it was just the sensation of being in my own skin.

That was the year I got the nickname Winnie Whore.

I didn't care then. I still don't care now.

And if Starla were here, she'd be telling me to use what I have.

"Most men don't realize this," she said once, "but us girls, we have toolboxes too. Ours aren't stuffed with hammers and wrenches and screwdrivers. We have these." She gave her boobs a squeeze. "And this." Then tapped at her temple. "And there's no greater power than tits and brains, baby girl."

The way Kas's gaze lingered on me...

If any of them are a weak link, it's him.

Can he take me home? Does he know how to leave the island? I'm sure I can get him on my side.

In the darkness of my room, an idea takes hold.

I sit up, clear my throat and call out for Kas. And within minutes, his footsteps sound outside my bedroom door and my heart leaps into my throat.

I'm going to fuck a Lost Boy.

9

KAS

If the Darling calls for me, I come.

Bash and I have been tasked as her keepers, as we always are.

For decades, we've looked after the Darlings.

Look, but don't touch.

I find her sitting up in bed crying.

Immediately I want to make her feel better.

Pan always says I am the bleeding heart out of the four of us.

"What is it?" I sit on the edge of the bed beside her.

"I'm scared," she says and collapses against me, her hand curled in my shirt. She sobs and I give in.

How can I not?

I pull her closer. Her body shakes.

I can just hear Bash in the back of my head—*this is a very bad idea.*

But I know what the fuck I'm doing.

I don't lose control like Vane and I sure as hell don't

indiscriminately fuck around like Bash. I can handle a weeping Darling without trying to fuck her.

"Winnie," I say, "it'll be all right."

"He's going to break me."

"No, he won't."

"Yes, he will. Just like he broke my mom."

Her tears wet my shirt. I can hear the rapid beat of her heart, can sense the pulsing rush of her blood in her veins.

Bash and I are not the same as Pan and Vane, but we are monsters, nonetheless.

She puts her hand on my thigh and sinks closer.

My cock takes notice.

"Darling," I say, my voice going husky and dark. "I should go."

"No. Wait." She tries to wrap her hand around my bicep, but she's too small. "I don't want to be alone."

My chest tightens.

"Please stay." Her voice is a whimper.

"For a minute," I tell her.

"Thank you."

We're quiet for a beat and the quiet needles at the back of my neck. "Do you want to see something?" I ask her.

She's suddenly on guard. "Like what?"

"Lie back."

The chain rattles as she does. The bed squeaks.

The Darling is too trusting. And I am straddling the line.

I lie down beside her.

Moonlight pours into the window behind us and stretches along the walls.

My magic always stirs on a full moon. Just like the tides, it grows in the light.

I don't even have to think about it as the illusion breaks open across the ceiling.

Beside me, the Darling gasps and I can't help but smile.

"What is that?" she asks.

The night sky appears above us in shimmering shades of black and blue and violet and stars twinkle in the darkness.

Some Darlings like the magic. Some don't.

Some think it's just a trick of the eye.

But it's all real.

Neverland is full of magic.

Or at least it was, once.

Now it's dying.

Which is the whole reason the Darling is here.

Save the king, save the island.

It's a ridiculous notion, all of these centuries later. Sometimes I forget that Pan is a king, that there's anything left to rule.

It will never go back to what it was before he lost his shadow.

I don't even know what we're fighting to get back anymore.

The magic, I suppose.

The land.

But for Pan, sometimes I think it's the power. He doesn't give a fuck about the hibiscus or the lilies or the cloudberry bushes.

A king cannot become something else. He will always be a king. Without the throne, he is nothing.

The Darling turns to look at me. The starlight above us brightens and I can't even hide that the illusion is tied to me.

The others hate when a Darling comes to Neverland. I've always enjoyed it.

It breaks up the monotony.

"What are you?" she asks.

I laugh, low and beneath my breath. "I am many things, Darling."

"But this" —she lifts her hand, gestures to the ceiling— "what is that? How can you do that?"

Bash and I don't talk about where we came from. Because we can never go home.

"In your world," I tell her, "I believe you might have called us fairies."

She laughs and the glimmering starlight plays across the line of her brow. "But I don't believe in—

I clamp my hand over her mouth and her startled breath rushes out around my fingers.

"Don't say it."

She frowns.

"Promise me you won't."

She gives me a quick nod, so I pull my hand away.

"Why not?" she asks. "You can't say you don't believe in—"

"Darling." Her name is a growl and my heart is racing in my ears. "If you say it, I'm dead."

"What?" The question is another trill of laughter. "That can't be true."

"Well, it is."

I am reminded of my mother suddenly. The cut of her wings, the glow of her skin.

"If you say those words, a fairy dies. It's as simple as that. So promise me you won't say it."

She resettles on the bed. "I promise."

I lie back down beside her.

"If you're a fairy, where are your wings?"

"I lost them." The admission is soaked in sorrow and filled with rage.

"What happened to them?"

I sigh. "That is a very long story."

She regards me with a furrowed brow. I think she thought this conversation would go in a much different direction.

"You said that in my world, you'd be called a fairy. What do they call you here?"

"Fae is a better word." We are not all creatures of stardust and light, not like my mother. The fae here are bathed in blood. But the fae have one rule: do not kill each other.

Bash and I broke that.

"And Pan?" the Darling asks.

"Is not fae."

"So what is he?"

I've dug myself too far. The starlight on the ceiling flickers and fades.

"Not my story to tell, Darling."

She huffs and readjusts beside me. The bed squeaks.

I like this Darling too much already. Maybe I don't know what I'm doing after all.

She turns to her side and tucks her hands beneath her head.

Beyond the house, the waves crash against the shore. I can taste a summer storm on the air.

"What about your tattoos?" She reaches across the space between us and traces a finger down one of the curved lines of my markings. "Do they mean something?"

"They did, once."

"And now?"

"Now they are just a reminder."

I shiver as she follows a line down my neck to the collar of my shirt. To the fae, the tattoos are a mark of rank and order. Bash and I were supposed to be significant.

Now we're a cautionary tale.

Her hand trails down my chest, down my stomach, and my abs constrict.

I'm suddenly fucking harder than stone.

Her hand sinks lower.

I snatch her wrist. "Don't."

"Don't what?"

"I know what you're doing."

"And what's that?"

"You're trying to cause tension in the group. You're not the first to think you're smarter than us. You're not, Darling. Whatever strategy you think you're plotting, we've seen it before. We've watched every move play out, and all of the Darlings bend. Eventually."

I want to fuck her just to teach her a lesson.

The tide comes in. My magic beats at my ribs.

We are all tied to the night in one way or another.

Dark creatures are best left to the dark nights.

"We don't touch the Darlings," I tell her and then get up.

"I wasn't...I mean..."

"Good night, Darling," I say and then leave the room, shut the door behind me.

When I readjust my cock, it almost hurts.

I need...*something*.

I go through the loft to the balcony. "Where are you going?" Bash calls.

"Out," I say.

The rest of the Lost Boys are sitting around the bonfire and there are a dozen girls from town. They are always desperate for the attention of the King and his men.

I pick one out. Any will do.

"You," I tell a girl with dark brown hair. "Get on your knees."

Her eyes go wide and she looks past me to the others.

"On your knees or leave. You choose."

She licks her lips then rises from the chair and sinks to the patio. She unzips my pants, pulls my cock out, strokes me in her hand.

Fuck.

The hair along the nape of my neck bristles as magic fills the air.

I can make anything appear real. Make any illusion real enough to touch.

But the one thing I can't do?

I can't pretend that I'm not as fucked up as the rest of them.

The girl takes me in her mouth. She's slow and gentle and unsure and I fucking hate it.

I bury my hand in her hair and shove down her throat. She gags. Tears fill her eyes. The others watch as I fuck her mouth, brutally, mercilessly.

She takes it.

Every inch.

And the whole time, I can't help but imagine it's the Darling's lips wrapped around my cock.

Maybe she knows what she's doing after all.

10

WINNIE

THE CHAIN THEY CUFFED ME TO IS JUST LONG ENOUGH FOR ME TO leave the bed and reach the bank of windows. The shutters are still open so I can hear everything going on down there.

I hear Kas tell a girl to get on her knees and she does it without question and the rest of them hanging out by the fire watch as he takes her.

Some weird, foreign feeling fills my chest as I watch.

I'm buzzing between my legs, suddenly wet.

I was going to do that. That should be me. Except watching him...

Why the hell am I so aroused by this?

The girl starts choking on him, but he doesn't give in.

I am entranced by him, by the thrusting of his hips and the glint of the moonlight on his dark hair, the straight dark lines of his tattoos and—

My bedroom door bangs open. A dark figure stalks in, grabs my chain and yanks me back. I lose my footing, stumble. Bash catches me and wraps a hand around my throat.

"What did you say to him, Darling?"

"What? I didn't—"

"I know my brother. He's my other half, after all."

There's just enough moonlight pouring through my windows to see the hard scowl on Bash's face. They may be identical, but Bash's edges are sharper.

He must be the older of the two, Kas's protector even though I doubt he needs protecting.

"I didn't do anything."

Bash's grip on me tightens. "All of you fucking Darlings are the same. You act innocent, like you're the victims—"

"We are!"

He snorts. "Keep telling yourself that."

"*You* kidnapped *me*. I don't want to be here!"

He swings me around and presses me against the wall. The air is knocked out of me.

"You think we want you here?" he says. "You think this is fun for us? Watching Pan slowly die right in front of our eyes? Feeling the island revolt as if it wants to spit us out? You think we asked for the Darlings to—"

He cuts himself off and takes in a long, deep breath, nostrils flaring.

"Pan is dying?" I say.

He scowls and his eye twitches.

"Why is he dying?"

He removes his hand from my throat, but it lingers on my shoulder, his thumb pressing at the valley between my collarbones.

I'm still ignited after watching his brother fuck some girl's mouth.

My heart is racing in my chest.

Bash meets my eyes and he narrows his.

His breathing quickens and I realize I made a mistake

trying to get to Kas first. I thought he would be the one because he was the nicest. But that's exactly the reason he wouldn't touch me. Not first, anyway.

Starla, I think, *I'll make you proud.*

You fuck the one that's good and ready, she'd say.

It wouldn't be the first time I've used my body to get what I want.

I let out a breathy little moan and Bash clenches his teeth together, presses closer. I can feel his cock hard against my thigh.

I push my hips forward, rock against him.

He growls.

Bash will fuck me.

I'm sure of it now.

And when he does, Kas will be pissed and Pan will be pissed and I'm not sure what Vane will do.

But I will have set something in motion.

Channeling my inner Starla, I reach between us and grope Bash and his nostrils flare as a rumble sounds deep in his chest.

I stroke him through his pants.

"Darling," he says, "you're playing with fire."

"Am I?"

His hand slides back up my throat as his teeth grit together.

I bring my hand up and steal in beneath the waistband of his pants. When I feel the heat of his cock, the head swells and I drag my thumb over the slit.

"Fuck it," he says and spins us around, sitting himself on the edge of the bed, me on his lap.

He has himself out before I can take a breath and then he's tearing my panties aside and shoving into me.

"Bounce on my cock, Darling," he orders and the triumph nearly escapes me in a high-pitched squeal.

I seat my knees on the bed, wrap my arms around him and slide him out, then back in. His grip is hard on my hips, driving me down on him. "Fuck. This is a bad idea."

"I think it's a brilliant idea."

He throbs inside of me.

I yank off his shirt.

If I'm going to use my body to get what I want, then I at least want to admire what I'm taking in return.

Bash is corded in muscle, covered in those deliberate dark lines. His abs constrict as he shoves into me.

"Fuck, Darling. Fucking hell. Pan is going to kill me."

He yanks down the collar of my dress, pulls my breast out and captures my nipple in his mouth. He bites at me. I yelp and jolt against him, but he tightens his hold on me.

Rocking my clit against him, my pleasure builds.

I'm fucking a Lost Boy.

I have a plan.

I'm going to get out of here and then—

I feel Peter Pan before I see him.

And when he walks in the room, Bash immediately goes still beneath me.

I see the flick of a lighter first, the flame dancing in the darkness, burning the end of the cigarette in his mouth.

Bash throbs deep inside of me.

Pan snaps the lighter shut with a definitive clack, then takes a pull on the cigarette, the bright ember burning neon orange.

When he exhales smoke, he says, "Don't stop on my account."

He comes into the room, sitting in the wingback chair behind me.

Bash exhales, almost a sigh. He's still hard, still buried in me, but he doesn't move.

"Go on," Pan says. "Fuck her."

"Pan...I didn't—"

"Fuck her, Bash. Do it now."

Bash looks up at me. I can't tell if there's regret or relief on his face.

He thrusts up, guides my hips down the length of him.

I can't see Pan, but I can feel his heavy gaze on my backside and somehow that is the most erotic thing I've ever experienced.

I like it more than I should. I might have fucked half the basketball team, but never at once.

Bash picks up the tempo and I help him along, bouncing on him as we get closer and closer and the room fills with curling smoke and the smell of burning tobacco.

My clit throbs, desperate for friction and I rock forward, grinding against Bash, sliding down the length of him.

"Fuck, Darling. Just like that."

He grows harder inside of me.

"Fuck. Fuck, yes."

His chest rises and falls and then all of the muscle in his body tenses up as he growls and slams into me, spilling cum inside of me.

I'm so close.

I just need a few more thrusts.

I pant into Bash's neck and hold on tight, coated in sweat now and warm summer air.

So close.

So close.

A strong arm wraps around my waist and yanks me off of Bash, stealing the pleasure and the heat.

I'm throbbing and wet and leaking cum.

"Get out," he tells Bash.

"For fuck's sake, Pan," Bash says as he yanks his pants up. "If you're trying to teach me a lesson, you missed the mark."

"Go on," Pan says with me still pressed against his chest.

When Bash is gone, Pan whirls me around and tosses me into the wingback. The chain rattles and grows taut.

He points a finger at me, silver ring flaring in the moonlight. "You don't know what the fuck you're getting yourself into."

"I was kidnapped. I think I know well enough."

He bristles.

Good. This is what I wanted. Get beneath their skin. Look for weaknesses.

This is my talent. I can do this.

I pull up the hem of my skirt. There's a dark, wet mark on my panties, both from my pussy and Bash's cum.

Pan can't help but look down between my legs. His jaw flexes as he hunches closer.

I pull my panties aside and slide my fingers down my wet slit, dip a fingertip inside of me.

I am enjoying this. Maybe more than I should.

I'm like a kid let loose at a county fair and I want to ride all the rides and play all the games.

What do I really have to lose?

Yesterday I didn't think any of this was real.

Maybe it's not.

Maybe this is all a dream and if it is, then I can do whatever the hell I want.

I moan as I rub at my clit.

Pan glares at me, his nearly-white eyes almost glowing in the moonlight.

I don't know what he is and I don't think I care.

All I know is that he's my captor and I'm not going to let him keep the upper hand.

I sink in the chair, spread my legs further and pick up the pace.

I was already primed to come before Pan yanked me away. I'm already *this* close.

I fight the urge to close my eyes and sink into the searing heat.

I want to see him when I come.

I want to know how he feels about it because regardless of what these boys are, I think I can still read them like an open book. And whatever words I read I will use against them later.

The anticipation of the orgasm sends a shiver down my spine and I arch in the chair, baring more of myself to him.

His gaze dips to my pussy as I work at my clit.

He's so hungry.

The searing heat between my legs nearly consumes me as his nostrils flare.

Peter Pan was a myth and now he's real and he's drinking in the sight of me like I'm a mirage.

As I descend into the pleasure, Pan's hand slides up my thigh and gooseflesh erupts on my skin.

Touch me, I think.

Touch me.

I slow my pace, hold my fingers over my clit trying to keep the orgasm at bay just to see what Pan will do.

He sinks two fingers inside of me all the way up to his first knuckle.

My breath gets stuck in my throat.

He slides his fingers back out slowly, then shoves in hard again, rocking me back against the chair.

I'm being finger fucked by a myth.

Oh my god.

"Don't stop, Darling," he orders.

I swirl my fingers around my clit, nerves blinking alive.

Pan pulls his fingers out of me and then shoves them into my mouth.

My eyes pop open. I can taste the sweetness of my juices and the tang of cum.

"Clean them off."

I run my tongue down the length of his fingers as he commands. His eyes narrow.

"What's that taste like?" he asks, then sets his jaw hard as he waits for me to answer.

"I...I don't know."

"Trouble," he tells me. "Filthy little Darling whore."

His words ignite something in me.

"Oh fuck," I say around a moan. "Yes."

I'm so hot, so wound up tight, descended so far into oblivion, that the wave crashes through me in an instant and my inner walls clench up and I hold my breath, my entire body tensing up.

I don't want it to end.

Heat floods through me and I pull into myself, toes curling. My knees draw up, but Pan knocks them back, keeps me spread open.

I pant out, breathless, a little dizzy.

I've been ignited like a supernova.

Pan grips me roughly by the jaw and forces me to look at him as sweat coats my forehead, my chest, as the breath wheezes out of me.

Fury has sharpened the planes of his face.

"We don't fuck Darlings," he tells me. "Stop fucking around or you will regret it."

And then he leaves me, soaking wet and dirty in the chair.

11

PETER PAN

I'M SO FUCKING HARD AND PISSED OFF THAT I COULD SPLIT THE Darling in two.

That wet cunt was just begging to be fucked.

She knew exactly what she was doing and she did it so well too.

I go outside to the balcony and light another cigarette. It's not enough. It's not what I want.

The smoke burning in my lungs unwinds some of the tension between my shoulder blades. I prop my hands on the stone railing. The other Lost Boys have scattered but the bonfire still burns in the pit.

Somewhere in the surrounding forest, a mockingbird calls out in the night as the wind shifts and the palm fronds rustle.

Vane finds me there when he comes up the stairs. He's been unwound too, more so than me. I can tell it by the energy in the air. I might not have all of my power, but at least I have that.

"You take care of it?" I ask him.

He gives me a nod, but his face tells me he didn't like it.

"Cherry?" I ask.

"Yeah."

"She survive it?"

"Barely."

"They never know what they're asking for." I'm not just talking about Cherry.

I take another hit, let the smoke leak out on its own.

"Cherry knew. But she asked for it anyway." Vane tips his chin at me. "What's got you looking like murder?"

I sigh. "Bash fucked the Darling."

And then I stuck my fingers inside of her.

I can still smell her on me every fucking time I bring the cigarette to my mouth. So sweet. So tempting.

"Christ." Vane leans against the railing, crosses his arms over his chest. "And you?" he asks.

I darken my gaze. "What about me?"

"I can smell her on you. I'm not a fucking idiot."

"I taught her a lesson."

"You teach yourself one too?"

I take one last hit and smash the cigarette in a nearby crystal bowl, blowing the smoke out with a breath.

"If this one is getting beneath your skin already," he says, "we're all in fucking trouble."

"Vane—"

"Don't let her."

"I fucking won't."

He levels his gaze at me, one violet eye, one black. His shadow is quiet, but I can sense it prowling beneath his skin. It is never totally satiated. Vane and his shadow hail from a different island, a darker one.

Even without the shadow, he'd be terrifying.

I still don't know how I convinced him to leave his island.

He never told me his story and I never asked.

But the longer he's here, the harder it is for him to contain what he is, the desires he has.

He's fighting a different battle than me, but we are each fighting, nonetheless.

"I'll be fine," I tell him.

He gives me a nod. "Don't stay out too long. The sun is about to break."

After he leaves, I linger on the balcony, hunched over the railing for much longer than I should.

The closer the sun gets to the horizon, the more my skin aches, the more my stomach churns.

We just have to keep it together long enough to get inside the Darling's head, root around inside her memories and see what we can see. Two more nights until the full moon.

We'll bide our time until then.

As the first ray of light peaks over the ocean horizon, I hesitate and drink in the color of day.

I get less than ten seconds before my skin is cracking and the pain surges through my veins, white hot and prickling.

Without my shadow, the daylight is a death knell.

I have to race to the tomb, smoke curling in my wake.

12

I WAKE THE NEXT MORNING WHEN THE SUN IS ALREADY HIGH IN the sky.

The air is warm but breezy and my windows stayed open all night, so the sunlight and the ocean air steals in easily.

If I wasn't kidnapped and ferried away to some distant island by a myth of a man and then chained to a bed, I'd actually feel like I was on the best vacation of my life.

The waves are a rhythmic rush and trickle against the rocks and beach sand. I pull the wingback over to one of the windows, get comfortable in the seat and then prop my bare feet on the windowsill.

I sit there for an hour just watching the gulls dart back and forth over the beach. There's no one outside and no one stirs beyond my room. I think this is a house of night owls.

As I sit, I can't help but daydream about what I did last night.

A tingling heat settles between my legs and I close my thighs together, trying to drive off the arousal.

I wanted to push a wedge in between the Lost Boys, but I might have enjoyed last night far more than I thought I would.

I liked being called a whore.

If Pan called me a whore and fucked me—

"Good morning."

I lurch upright as Cherry comes in.

"Hell," I say. "You scared me."

"Sorry," she says. She comes to the bed and sets down a tray of food.

"What happened to you?" I ask her as I get up. There are scratches on her face and bruises on her arms.

"I fell down."

"Where? In a barrel of broken glass?"

She ignores me. "I made you fresh coffee. Do you use cream or sugar?"

Beside the coffee, there's a plate with toast and a bowl of fruit.

"Some cream would be nice."

She removes the lid from one of the cups and pours in thick cream. The coffee pales.

"Did you sleep well?" she asks.

Oddly enough, yes, I did. Better than I have in a long time.

"Eat," Cherry says. "I picked the berries fresh this morning. The bush didn't produce much, but then it rarely does. So these are gold around here. Just so you know."

I come over to sit on the giant bed. The chain comes with me. Cherry frowns at it.

"You don't like my new jewelry?" I ask her and lift my arm with a flourish. "It's very avant-garde."

She laughs. She has a tinkling laugh that reminds me of Christmas and snow globes and elves.

I pluck a berry from the bowl and pop it in my mouth. Cherry watches me.

"You're very pretty," she says.

"I know," I say.

She frowns at me.

"It's best you know what your assets are," I say, almost a parrot of Starla.

Cherry shakes her head. "I don't know if I have any."

"Sure you do." I fold my legs beneath me and take a sip of the coffee. It's honestly the best cup I've ever had. Better than Starbucks.

Why does everything taste better here?

"Your hair and your freckles are an asset," I tell Cherry. "And you have this innocent look about you. Can you be devious?"

She laughs nervously. "I don't think so."

"I bet they underestimate you."

She knows who I'm talking about.

"I..." She looks down at the sheet tangled at the end of my bed. "I don't have magic or power. So I don't think there's anything to underestimate."

Hand curled around the coffee mug, I bring it halfway, but watch her through the steam.

She's lonely and desperate for attention. Something I suspect the Lost Boys will never give her.

I can give her attention. Just one more thing I can use when I need to.

"Who is your favorite?" I ask and take another sip of the coffee. God, it feels good to have something normal. Even though I haven't been here long, everything is different. I need something that's not.

"Of the boys?" she asks.

"Yes."

A smile plays over her mouth and she ducks her head.

"Go on," I coax. "Spill the secrets."

"Well..."

"Yes?"

"Vane."

I grimace with bared teeth. "Seriously?"

She blushes and tucks a lock of her auburn hair behind her ear. "There's just something about him—"

"Scintillating and psychotic?"

"It's his shadow. He—"

"Wait...his what?"

She licks her lips. Shit, I've caught her in something she wasn't supposed to say.

That's exactly why I need to befriend her.

I lower my voice. "I won't say anything. Promise."

She checks the door, then leans into me, excited to have a secret that I don't. "There are more islands than Neverland. Seven islands, seven kings. Every island has two shadows. One for life, one for death. The king always claims a shadow. It's in his blood, having the ability to claim it." Her voice thins as she grows more excited. "The king picks which one he wants. Pan picked life a very long time ago. But when Pan lost his shadow, he lost the power and now the island is suffering because of it and I think Pan might be dying."

I blink at her.

It's a lot to take in.

"So Pan is a king?" I ask.

"Yes. Or he was. But that was before I was born."

"And he lost his shadow?"

"Yes."

A puzzle piece clicks into place.

He thinks the Darlings took his shadow. He said as much without saying it exactly.

He's going to have a hard time getting that information out of me considering I've literally never heard of it and definitely don't know how to find it.

It makes my plan even more important. Because if I can't give him what he wants...

"What about the death shadow or whatever from this island?" I ask.

She shakes her head. "It's been missing for a very long time. No one has seen it and no one seems interested in finding it. Death shadows are nothing to be messed with."

Her gaze goes distant as she says this and I get the distinct impression she knows more about death shadows than she's letting on.

"Last night, Kas was telling me about the fae and that he and Bash are fae, but they lost their wings?"

Cherry nods. "They killed their father."

"What?!"

And here I thought the twins were the nicer ones.

"Killing another fae is grounds for banishment and losing their wings. That's why they're here with Pan and the Lost Boys. They were banished from the fae court."

"Court?"

All of this information is making my head spin, but I'd be lying if I said it didn't excite me too. This is all so interesting. It's better than a TV show.

"And you?" I ask. "What are you?"

"Me?" Her voice is squeaky when she says the word. "I'm human. I...I come from the north end of the island. Hook's territory."

"And who is Hook?"

"Captain of the pirates."

"And the pirates—"

"Hate Pan."

"Right."

"They want to take over the island." She fidgets with a loose thread on the white sheets. Wraps it around the end of her finger until it turns blue.

"Do they have a shot at it?"

She focuses on a distant spot on the wall, but I don't think she's looking at it so much as disappearing into a memory. "Maybe. Maybe not. My—Hook—is relentless."

She knows Hook personally. But how?

"Have you ever left the island? Do you know how to... cross worlds, I guess?"

She shakes her head, unwinds the string from around her finger and the blood rushes back in.

I set the coffee cup down and collapse back against the pillows. "Just as well. I guess I'm stuck chained to this bed, bored out of my goddamn mind."

"Well," Cherry says, "maybe I can talk the twins into letting you come down to the bonfire tonight. Just to get you out of the house."

"Okay. That could be fun."

I can just imagine all of the trouble I could cause at a bonfire.

My brain conjures an image of Kas fucking that girl's mouth last night and my stomach lights up and then the sensation dips between my legs.

There's something about seeing the supposed nice guy act not so nice.

"I'll ask Bash. He'll likely say yes," Cherry says. "Kas will be harder to come around, but what Bash wants, Kas usually gives him."

And vice versa, I bet.

"And Pan and Vane?"

She rolls her eyes. "Even less so than the twins."

"Something tells me they're the guys who pop balloons at a kids' party."

She laughs. "You're funny, Darling."

"Thanks."

"Enjoy your breakfast. I'll be back later," she says and slides off the bed.

"Cherry?"

"Hmm?"

"Did Vane give you those cuts and bruises?"

It's really none of my business, but I have to know.

She bites at her bottom lip before giving me a nervous laugh. "It comes with the territory."

"Which is what?"

"Vane has a shadow too. From another island."

I think I know what she's going to say before she says it.

"And his shadow is death."

13

BASH

Kas and I are in the hammocks strung up between palm trees down by the beach. I haven't told Kas yet about the trouble I caused last night.

Using a long stick, he shoves off the ground, getting the hammock to swing again. Then he pushes me with it, jamming the stick into my ass.

"Fucker," I say.

He laughs.

A gull dares to come closer, hoping we have some scraps to give, but I only have a length of rope in my hands. Tying knots soothes me.

"I have to tell you something," I say to my twin.

The rope hammock groans beneath Kas as he resettles. "I'm listening."

"I fucked the Darling."

He's suddenly silent, but the hammock still creaks. Another wave laps against the shore. A sand fly lands on my arm and I smack it beneath my palm, smashing guts on my skin.

"When should I start planning your funeral?" Kas finally says.

"Very funny."

"He'll kill you. Surprised he hasn't yet."

I take a handful of white sand from the ground beneath me and grind it against my arm, cleaning off the guts.

"What happened?" he asks.

"Pan caught us and told me to keep fucking her. Honestly, I think the Darling liked it."

My cock twitches, remembering the feel of her tight little pussy. I've never given in to a Darling before, as much as I've wanted to. I like fucking. I like fucking what I shouldn't even more.

"How was she?" my twin asks.

I'm hard now, aching for more.

"Slutty, just the way I like them."

He blows out a breath. "You're such a fucking asshole."

"Yeah, well, the whole reason I went into her room last night was because of you."

"You keep telling yourself that."

Up the hill, I can just make out Cherry crossing the balcony and scanning the beach. When she spots us, she comes down.

I'm not in the mood for Cherry.

I'm not sure I've ever been.

Unlike the Darling, I've always had free access to Cherry. Takes away some of the fun.

"Hi," she says when she comes up. "Can Winnie come to the bonfire tonight?"

Kas gives me another gentle push with the stick. "Why?" he asks.

"I thought it might be good for her while we wait for the full moon."

"Pan will say no."

Cherry puts her hands on her hips. "We have a bonfire every night. Since when do we need his permission?"

"We don't," I say, "but he'll certainly have an opinion about the Darling attending."

"I'll take care of Pan."

Kas laughs at the sky. "Just what the fuck do you think you're going to say to Peter Pan to make him bend to you?"

"He's not as unreasonable as you both make him out to be." She squints as the wind shifts and the palms break open allowing the sun to stream in. "Besides, where is she going to go? There's nowhere to run."

"Looks like you did plenty of running last night," I say.

Kas frowns at me and says, *Stop teasing her.*

Why, when it's so easy to get her flustered?

"Stop doing that," she says.

"Doing what?"

"Talking in your fae language. I can hear the bells, but not the words and it annoys me." She huffs.

"We were just discussing the Death Shadow is all," I lie. "Did it give you the best, most terrifying orgasm of your life, Cherry?"

Her face pinks.

To be honest, I'm surprised she's upright and walking.

When Vane's shadow takes over, it fucking terrifies *me* and he's not trying to fuck me.

"I'm not talking about my sex life with you two anymore," she says. Then, "So can she?"

"I suppose," I say. "You know how much I love pretty girls and parties."

"Because you're a self-absorbed prick," Kas says.

"He's not wrong," I tell Cherry.

"Will you make the food?" she asks me.

"Is there anyone better?" I don't wait for her to answer. "No. There's not. So yes, I'll make the food."

"Good. Let's say seven."

"I thought you were going to ask Pan first? The sun doesn't set till eight-thirty at the earliest."

She smirks. "I *will* ask him. For forgiveness."

"Brave little Cherry," I say. "Fine. Now go away."

She rolls her eyes, then starts back up the hill, disappearing through the palm fronds.

"You think you can keep your dick in your pants tonight?" Kas asks.

"Doubtful."

He pokes me with the stick again. I snatch it from his grasp and whack him with it.

He laughs and rubs the sore spot. "If you get us kicked out of the treehouse, we'll have nowhere else to go. So behave yourself."

"Pan doesn't kick people out. He *thins* them out. If Pan grows tired of us, we're dead. So really I don't know why you're worried."

He grumbles to himself.

I close my eyes and sink back into the hammock. The ropes tied around the tree creak. We're quiet again and then Kas says, "Tilly will be here tomorrow night."

"I know."

"I miss our sister."

I sigh. "I do too." And the palace. And the court drama. I thrived in that place.

"You think she'll ever forgive us?"

"I don't think so."

It's hard to forgive your brothers when they gutted your

father right in front of you.

"You know what I've been wondering about since Merry?" Kas asks.

"What's that?"

"I wonder if our dear sister is really doing what she claims to be doing with the Darlings."

Now my eyes are wide open. "You think she's lying to Pan?"

Kas turns in the hammock so his feet are in the sand. "What if she is? What would we do about it?"

"That is a loaded question."

"I know it is."

We drop it then and there.

I think we're both afraid of the answer.

14

BROWNIE

THE BROWNIE HAS NO NAME.

He is older than most on the island, but not older than Peter Pan.

Even the Brownie is unsure of where Pan came from or what he is.

It's undeniable that he is connected to the island, that both he and the land have laid a claim on one another.

Which explains why the island's energy is like a buzzing wasp nest that's been whacked with a stick.

The Brownie remembers when Pan was king and he doesn't wish to return to what Neverland was when it was under his rule, but if they are to be rid of him, they have to have a plan.

The Brownie set one in motion a very long time ago with Tinker Bell, stars rest her soul.

Hurrying through the underground fae palace, the Brownie's leather shoes are silent on the rough stone floor.

The walls are webbed in vines. The vines are dotted with primroses and honeycaps and bright pink hibiscus flowers. The air smells of sweet fae wine and chimes with court gossip.

When he enters the throne room, the Brownie finds Queen Tilly at a large round table sharing tea with several other noble fae. A golden circlet has been woven into her dark hair. One single ruby glitters in the centermost tine. Tilly looks like an eighteen-year-old girl, but she is older too.

Everyone on Neverland is older than they look.

The fae don't age like mortals do, but even the mortals have escaped the toll of time, what with the Death Shadow gone.

"What is it?" she asks when she sees him.

When the Brownie is seen, there is always an "it."

"Peter Pan has the Darling," he answers.

"Leave us," she says quickly and the others scatter.

The Brownie waits for the queen to command him, his hands clasped behind his back.

Once the room is empty save for himself and Tilly, she turns to him. "This Darling... She's Merry's daughter, isn't she?"

"Yes."

Tilly paces the length of the throne room. It takes her three minutes total. It's a very large room. "Tell me your thoughts."

The Brownie crosses the room to come to stand beside her in the bright glow of a pixie bug lantern. "He's losing the island. I can feel it."

Tilly nods. "And?"

"And I don't think he'll get his chance at another Darling."

She nods again and worries at the inside of her cheek. "He'll summon me soon and I'll do what I've always done. No more, no less."

"Forgive me for speaking out of turn, my queen, but if you wanted the island, now would be the time to take it."

She regards him down the sharp slant of her nose. She got her mother's cat-like features, but her father's warrior's eyes. She is the fiercest queen that's ever ruled the fae on Neverland. The Brownie is glad to serve her.

But she could do so much more.

"What would your mother want?" the Brownie asks.

"Tink loved Pan once," she says.

"Yes, and he killed her. Don't make her death be in vain."

"Don't tell me what I should or shouldn't do, Brownie."

"Of course, my queen. But..." Compared to the Brownie, the queen is but a baby. Sometimes it's exhausting trying to coax her into action. "Perhaps we could use your brothers to—"

"Absolutely not."

The Brownie clamps his mouth shut. The twins have always been a sore spot. But they are an asset they could use if they wanted to unseat the king.

"I don't have to do anything," the queen says. "I just have to bide my time like I have been. Peter Pan will fail because I will make him fail. He will crumble and then I will claim his shadow and the throne will rightfully be mine."

"And the twins?" the Brownie asks.

The queen wants to pretend that she has no love left for her older brothers, but the Brownie knows better.

Every time someone mentions them, she is gutted all over again, just like their father.

It's why she's forbidden anyone from speaking their names.

"I don't care what my brothers do," she says and walks away. "In the meantime, find out where Hook stands. I don't want to fight him too."

Then the queen is gone and the Brownie takes action.

15

WINNIE

An hour after Cherry leaves me, Kas comes to my room and unchains me. He's wearing a shirt today, much to my disappointment.

Several tines of his black ink stick out from the collar of his shirt. "If you promise to stay nearby," he says, "I'll leave you unchained."

I give him an innocent look. "Peter Pan already warned me there's nowhere to go."

He nods.

"I'm going to use the bathroom," I say.

"I'll wait. I wanted to talk to you."

When the bathroom door is shut behind me, I go to the vanity and look at myself in the mirror.

I look the same—pale skin, big green eyes, dark hair. I look the same, but I don't feel the same.

Reaching out with my hand, I touch the patinaed glass. It's cool beneath my touch and a little flash of relief warms in my gut.

I use the bathroom, then splash cold water on my face. When I come back out, Kas is in the wingback, his elbow on the arm, his hand curled around his strong jaw.

Something is troubling him. I can feel it.

I'm familiar with anxiety. That building feeling that your insides want to crawl to the outside and burst into flames.

Or at least that's how it is for me.

I sit on the end of the bed. "What's up?"

I may have only been held captive for two days, but Kas feels safe and comfortable already. I think it's because he had a very clear opportunity to fuck me last night and didn't.

He really is the nice one.

"My brother told me about last night," he says.

"Ahh, yes."

"I'm sorry he did that."

"Don't be."

He frowns at me.

"I like sex, Kas. I'm not afraid of it."

He sits forward, clasps his hands together. "You were kidnapped and chained to a bed."

"Which made it that much more enjoyable." I smile sweetly at him.

He sighs.

Kas doesn't know that being chained to a bed is the least of what I've suffered. I pull the collar of my sweater up so he doesn't see my scars.

"We're not supposed to touch the Darlings," he says, his voice taking on a harder edge. "Bash knows that and he broke the rule anyway because he's an arrogant, selfish prick."

"Oh, just my type."

Kas's dark brow furrows.

I laugh and he finally catches the joke.

"All right. Fine. I'm glad you're taking this so well."

If only he'd watched me take it last night.

Gods, I liked Pan watching. I'd liked it more than I probably should have.

The memory, still so vivid, comes back to me and heat sinks to my clit.

I'm suddenly starving for something that doesn't go in my belly.

Goosebumps run up my arms and I rub my hand over my sweater, trying to drive away the excited chill.

"Cherry wants you to come to the bonfire tonight. Do you want to come?"

"Peter Pan is okay with it?"

Kas makes a little cringe with his puffy lips. To think of those lips on my—

Good god, I'm a captive here and all I can think about is these boys taking me.

What is wrong with me?

I thought I was going to go mad yesterday. This is far better.

I'll take this any day of the week.

Maybe I am just a kid that's been let loose in a carnival.

"I take it that's a no?" I ask.

"He's still in his tomb so he doesn't know. It's debatable how he'll feel about it when he wakes."

"Then we should be good and drunk by then just to be safe."

He laughs again and watches me with an intensity that makes my insides soar. "You're different than the others," he says, his voice low, catching.

"Am I?"

He nods. "We're always prepared for screaming and sobbing and begging when a Darling comes. You're just sitting here pretending like you're on vacation."

"Oh? This isn't a resort?"

"See what I mean?" He scratches at the back of his head. His long hair is still tied up in a bun. I wonder how long it is when it's let loose. He is gorgeous in his own right. Different from Pan and Vane. They're all gorgeous.

It makes the basketball team look like a bunch of ferrets.

"Wait, did you say Pan was in his tomb?"

Kas winces.

"Why is he in a tomb?"

"A conversation for another day. If you're hungry, Bash is in the kitchen."

"You guys like feeding me."

His gaze wanders over my body. "You look like you need feeding."

It's all fun and games until they notice your fault lines, until they pry them open and peer inside.

"Didn't I tell you? I'm secretly an assassin. Makes it easier to get into tight spaces."

He frowns at me. "You don't have to do that."

"Do what?"

"Pretend. This island has been pretending for far too long." He turns for the door. "Come out when you're ready." And then he's gone.

I sit with his words for a while.

The problem is, I don't know how to stop pretending.

When I come out into the kitchen, I find Bash alone.

Late sunlight is pouring through the windows and in the distance, it's painting the ocean in shimmering strokes of gold and pink.

Bash is at the counter whipping things together in a bowl. He's shirtless and all of the muscles and tendons in his arms and across his chest are moving in sync in a way that is almost hypnotizing.

He's clearly the cook in the house, but I don't think there's much fat on him. He is cut like stone.

"Good morning, Darling," he says and looks up while he stirs.

"Afternoon, you mean?"

"Close enough." He winks at me while a lock of his black hair falls over his forehead.

"What are you making?"

"Honeysuckle tarts."

"They sound delicious."

"They will be."

I slide onto one of the stools across the island from him. "You think highly of yourself, don't you?"

"If you are not the most interesting person you know, then you're doing it wrong."

I arch a brow. "Some would call that narcissism."

"If you don't hold yourself on a pedestal, then who will?"

I reach over the island and stick my finger in the batter.

"Darling," he says and tsk-tsks at me. "Good girls wait their turn."

His gaze has darkened.

My belly dips and my pussy clenches.

Well.

I suck my finger into my mouth and clean it off.

He doesn't take his eyes off of me.

His jaw clenches and then he sets the bowl down, dips his finger into it, and reaches across the island. "Looks like I need mine cleaned off too."

Fuck. I've played this game before, but never with someone like Bash.

Usually I'm the one baiting the hook. Not the other way around. I don't know what to do with myself. I suddenly feel naive and out of my depth.

And I think it might be the way Bash is looking at me, like I am a toy to be played with.

I lift myself up from the stool so I can lean over the island to meet him.

I pop open my mouth and Bash slides his finger into me. I roll my tongue over him, cleaning off the sweet batter and he inhales sharply through his nose, teeth grinding together.

"Fuck, Darling," he whispers. "You're going to get me killed."

I pull my lips back, swirl my tongue over the end of his finger.

He visibly trembles and I am soaring high on the power and the pleasure of being pleasing.

Footsteps approach and Bash pulls back and deflates.

I look over my shoulder to see Vane in all of his menacing glory. He scowls at us, then looks at Bash's outstretched hand with his good eye, the violet one.

He's shirtless too, covered in black ink and when he comes around the island, I make out the dark shape of a massive skull with fangs tattooed on his back.

Side by side, Bash and Vane are close to the same

height, but Vane has an inch or two on him putting him well over six feet, I'd guess.

Bash is definitely stockier. Vane is all deep, shadowed lines, wiry like a brutal fighter.

He sticks two fingers into the batter, causing Bash to frown at him and then Vane silently comes around the island to me and wipes his sticky fingers over my mouth.

It catches me off guard and I inhale sharply.

When he steps back, the batter drips from my chin.

"That's better," he says and sets his jaw as if he's daring me to react.

Fury writhes up my spine. I've never been violent, but I think I could change my mind for Vane.

But that's exactly what he wants, isn't it?

He wants to get a rise out of me. They all do, in their own way.

Taking in a deep breath, I run my tongue over my bottom lip and swipe away the mess. "Mmmm," I say. "So good."

Frustration is a flicker in his good eye.

I give him the same show I gave Bash and swipe up the last of the mess with my index finger, then stick it in my mouth and practically fuck myself with it.

And then Vane's violet eye turns black.

I stumble back. He advances on me.

"Vane," Bash says.

Vane grabs me by the back of the neck and drives me into the island, bending me over the counter, forcing my face to the cool stone. I huff out a breath as he presses against my ass and leans over me, his voice at my ear.

"Do you want to know what I do to pretty little girls like you?"

His voice is rough and rumbling, the kind of voice you

only hear in horror movies coming out of the throats of monsters.

The terror slithers up my back, across my shoulders.

I can't stop the whimper from coming out of my throat.

"*Vane*," Bash says again.

Vane is hard at my ass, digging into me and my heart leaps, tangling with the pulsing terror.

I'm scared out of my mind and turned on more than I should be and I don't know what that says about me.

Vane's grip on my neck turns punishing.

"You wouldn't last ten minutes with me," he says.

"Okay, she gets it," Bash says.

"Does she? Do you, Darling?"

Heat sinks to my clit and instinctively, I arch my back, pushing my ass into him. His hand snakes around to my front and covers my mound.

My knees buckle, but Vane's grip is sure and he's not letting me go down.

My brain is saying I need to get out of this, find safety, but my body is saying more, more, *more*.

I haven't felt this way in a long time.

Like I am firmly in my body. And enjoying every second of it.

I've had so much sex I can't count the times, but I've never been in the hands of someone who knows what they're doing.

Vane's fingers rub at my clit and I think he might be punishing me more with pleasure than with pain.

I pant out against the counter.

He shifts his grip on me and my panties slide over my heat and the sensation makes me sag against the counter.

More.

More.

But suddenly he's gone.

And this time I do hit the floor.

"Darling," Bash says as he darts around the counter to crouch beside me.

"I'm okay."

He scoops me up effortlessly and keeps an arm around my waist. I'm still burning with heat, trembling with desire. My panties are soaked now.

I look up at Vane. His violet eye has returned to that bright shade of purple.

This wasn't about the terror this time.

It was about the art of the tease.

Showing me what he could do with so little effort.

I suck in a deep breath and fix my skirt. Bash is warm and solid at my side.

Vane regards me with cool indifference and I know he wants me to cry or beg.

So I do the opposite.

"Are all of you allergic to shirts?"

Bash snorts and buries a laugh.

Vane simmers.

He's not going to get to me.

He's already underestimated me.

He gives me one more snarling scowl and then turns and walks away.

"I can't believe you just did that," Bash says.

"Why?"

"Because Vane doesn't walk away from anyone. He punishes. He dominates. He does not relent."

"First time for everything, right? I mean, this is my first kidnapping so we're all having firsts."

He laughs again and shakes his head. "Where did you come from, Winnie Darling?"

"As if you don't know."

He narrows his eyes as he sizes me up. "Even if Pan doesn't find what he's looking for, I will be glad you were here. Shake things up. The gods know we could use it around here. Everyone is so damn broody."

"I guess I will take that as a compliment."

He winks at me. "It's certainly intended as one."

While Bash makes the food, Kas shows up with Cherry in tow. They're carrying matching wood-slatted crates. Inside, glass bottles clink together.

"More liquor?" I ask as they set the crates on the table. "You have an entire bar in the other room."

Cherry grabs a tall, skinny bottle with a deep red liquid inside. "The bottles on the bar are from your world and they're Pan's personal collection." She shows me the bottle in her hand. "This is faerie wine."

I've read stories about innocent young things drinking faerie wine and being trapped or corrupted by it. Some of those stories said once you've had faerie wine, you have no hope of ever going home.

But Cherry is human and she seems okay.

"Can I try some?" I ask.

Kas opens a cupboard and brings out several glasses, sets them on the counter. Down below, on the back patio, the party is already well underway. Music and laughter filters in and it reminds me of all of the high school parties I've attended over the years. And if I don't look at it too closely, I can almost pretend that this is a normal night, in a normal life.

Kas pops the cork from the bottle with nothing but his

bare hands and then tips the bottle over the glasses. The wine makes a glug-glug sound.

Cherry takes two glasses and hands one to me. "Go easy on it. It's a strong blend."

Bringing the wine to my nose, I inhale deeply. I've been drunk before, but usually on cheap vodka we drank straight from the plastic pint bottle. Me and Anthony and several of his friends.

I can smell cinnamon and cloves and maybe oranges in the wine.

I look up and find them all watching me.

"What? Is this a trick?"

Cherry laughs and shakes her head. "It's just that it's been a long time since we've had someone here from your world and I promise you, you've never tasted anything like faerie wine."

Well, here goes nothing.

I take a long sip and let the wine roll around on my mouth.

And it's...*wow*. Flavor blooms on my tongue. I can taste the oranges and the spices, but there's something tart, maybe cherries or maybe cranberries. It's a riot in my mouth as the alcohol brings heat near the end and I swallow it down.

My eyes are wide. The twins laugh at me.

"Holy shit," I say.

"See!" Cherry raises her glass and takes a long drink from hers.

Kas and Bash tip their glasses back and empty theirs in one swallow.

Already I'm warm all over.

Cherry refills us all, then, "Come on. Let's go down by the fire."

"Careful with our Darling," Kas says.

Cherry sighs. "Of course I will."

Our Darling.

Am I theirs?

Just the idea ignites a strange sort of flame in my gut. I've never been anyone's. Not even my mother's. She might have birthed me and did the best she could putting a roof over our heads, but she was never capable of being a mother.

The thought of belonging to someone is foreign and oddly gratifying.

Cherry clasps my hand in hers and pulls me out the double doors to the balcony. The ocean glitters with more color as the breeze lifts the hair from the back of my neck. The balcony is high off the ground and sits above the lower lying trees while the palm trees stand higher but are sparser.

This place is so beautiful.

I never gave Neverland much thought while my mom ranted about it. I never wanted to believe in it.

But she was right—there is magic here. There's magic in the beauty of it. And real magic too.

Down below, a fire is burning in the stone fire pit and there are easily two dozen people down there, most of them my age. Or at least, they appear to be my age.

There's a spirited card game going on at a round table and on the other side of the bonfire, a boy is playing the ukulele beside another boy with a guitar.

"Where did all of these people come from?" I ask.

Cherry pulls me over to the railing so we can look down on the party while we talk. Flickering lanterns hang from wrought iron hooks dotted around the clearing.

"This house is massive," Cherry explains. "You're

staying in what's known as the loft. Vane, Kas, and Bash live up there. The rest of the Lost Boys live on the main floor. There are a lot. I honestly can't even tell you how many."

"But where do they come from?"

She shrugs. "From town. From your world. From Hook's side. Lots of places. Lost Boys are just misfits, the ones who don't belong or who never wanted to grow up."

"Do they have magic too?"

"Not usually, no. Pan doesn't let the fae in. Bash and Kas are an exception."

I look over my shoulder and through the glass door to the kitchen. Kas is explaining something with his arms held wide and Bash is laughing at him.

There's more to their story, I'm realizing. And I desperately want to know it.

"I keep hearing about this town. Where is it?"

"That way." Cherry points back toward the kitchen and I'm assuming far beyond it. "But Pan probably won't let you go there."

"How big is this island?"

The guitar player picks a more upbeat tune and the ukulele adjusts to the beat.

"Pretty big. It would take you a half day to get to the other end by foot."

So maybe like ten miles across if I had to guess.

That at least gives me something to wrap my head around.

"Come on." Cherry starts for the stairs, but I linger at the balcony railing.

Several vines have taken hold in the stone and bright purple roses bloom from them, perfuming the air with a heady, sweet scent.

Two days ago I was terrified of going mad just like my mother and now I'm on an island in some other realm —*allegedly*—surrounded by the fae and vicious boys drinking faerie wine.

How quickly and suddenly things can change.

But I still don't want to go mad and I think that whatever Pan means to do to get inside my head is exactly how it happens.

It makes me wonder what my mom went through when she came here. Pan made it clear that he and the Lost Boys never touch the Darlings, but clearly, they did something to them. Otherwise there wouldn't be a legacy of insanity in my family tree.

Can I help him find his shadow without subjecting myself to the brain melt?

I take another sip of the wine and it immediately goes to my head and loosens the knots between my shoulders.

Alcohol makes everything better.

I drain my glass and return to the boys and hold out my cup.

Kas eyes me, considering.

"Please?" I say and give him an innocent stare.

Bash laughs and shakes his head.

"Fine." Kas uncorks the bottle and gives me a generous pour. That same flame returns at the thought of anyone caring what I do or don't do and it makes me want to test the strength of it, see how taut I can make it.

"Thank you." I smile at Kas and whirl around and go on the hunt for Cherry. I'm beginning to like this place. Maybe more than I should.

Cherry and I are playing cards with some of the Lost Boys. I don't know their names and they never asked mine. The boy beside me is short with red hair and he smells like cigarettes and mischief.

His hand is beneath the table, resting on my thigh. Everyone is handsy here, I'm realizing, and I'm pretty sure there was a couple fucking on the other side of the patio just a little bit ago.

This is a place of wild debauchery, a carnival ride that you never want to exit.

I've always loved carnivals.

The rides and the mischief.

The boy's hand slips further up my thigh and my skirt rides up and I giggle with excitement.

I don't know how much wine I've drunk. It doesn't seem like enough, but maybe it's been too much.

"Gable!" Cherry yells and slaps her cards on the table. The others groan.

Gable is a card game that I don't understand and that I keep losing. But it doesn't matter. I'm having the time of my life.

Kas and Bash joined the party an hour ago with food, and platters have been passed around with the cutest little tarts and gingersnaps that make my tongue burn.

Why was I ever afraid of coming here?

I could get lost in this world and never want to be found.

The boy edges closer and I glow beneath his attention. This is always where I'm most in my body, when someone else is touching it, when my nerves are awake. It's hard sometimes to feel anything at all.

Cherry laughs and falls off her chair and the boy beside her helps her back up.

My red-haired wonder pulls me onto his lap and his cock presses hard at my center.

He's no Bash or Kas and he's certainly no Pan, but he'll do just fine.

I lean into him and kiss him.

16

PETER PAN

I'M PULLED FROM SLEEP BY SOMEONE KICKING MY BED.

"This better be important."

"The twins are throwing a party," Vane says. "And the Darling is drunk."

I lurch upright, a foreign emotion burning in my chest.

"The fuck."

"I know. That's what I said."

"Why didn't you stop them? Or her for that matter?"

"I'm not her babysitter."

"Vane, for fuck's sake." I toss the sheet back as he flicks on the bedside lamp and the light immediately makes my vision burn. I stumble to the corner to fetch my clothes. I'm in a rush to get upstairs, but there is still sunlight in the air. I can feel it.

"How drunk is she?" I ask and pull on my pants.

I swear to god, if any of those assholes touches her—

Vane shrugs. "She was on the lap of one of the new Lost Boys when I came down."

A growl rumbles in my chest.

Vane narrows his eyes, regarding me with distant apprehension.

He is seeing something that neither of us recognizes.

I toss on a shirt and go to the door, hand poised to yank it open as I count down the seconds to the last drop of light.

"Think about what you're about to do," Vane says lazily behind me.

"You should have been watching her."

"Why do we care if she fucks a Lost Boy anyway?"

"I care."

"Why?"

I bow my head and take in a breath. I don't have a good fucking answer for that and the silence is telling.

Why do I care? The rule about not touching Darlings only pertains to myself and Kas and Bash and Vane. Because we are the only ones that matter. I don't give a fuck what the other Lost Boys do.

So the question stands—why do I care?

I don't know. I don't know why.

Fucking a Darling has nothing to do with getting inside her head.

It's the inherited memories I need. Not the pretty little Darling cunt.

"You're being rash," Vane says. "You do have a habit of being rash, but right now, I don't understand it and I don't like it." He presses his back to the wall beside the door and picks at his nails. "Maybe pause for a second and consider the options—"

The sun sinks below the horizon and I yank the door open.

"All right. Violence it is." He follows me up the stairs. I take them two at a time.

And the whole way up, his voice is a singing lilt behind me.

"Three, two, one. One, two, three. Better watch out: Peter Pan is going to murder thee."

The doors that lead to the patio are thrown open and music filters in.

I go there and scan the crowd of Lost Boys, the freshness of the night still bright enough that the lanterns are just a hazy glow.

I spot the Darling across the patio straddling some red-haired boy.

Her chest is in his face and he's gazing up at her, starry-eyed and hungry.

That knot returns to my chest.

I am blind with rage.

Some of the others see me and shrink away so that the crowd parts as I stalk through it.

The nameless Lost Boy sees me coming and he frowns.

Then he looks at the girl again and a dawning comes to his bloodshot eyes as horror washes over him.

"Oh, shit. Pan, I didn't know—"

I yank the Darling away and toss her into Vane's arms.

"Hey!" she yells.

I barely have magic, but I do have *power*.

So when I grab the back of the boy's chair and punch at his chest, I go straight through bone, claw my fingers around his heart and tear it out.

Blood sprays, painting the night in spots of crimson.

When it splatters across my face, I finally exhale, and the urgency ebbs away.

The party is silent as the blood patters to the stone.

The boy slumps over in the chair, eyes wide and dead.

When I turn back to the Darling, a heart in my hand, her eyes are full of tears.

Good.

She needs to know...there are no white knights here.

Just monsters.

And I am the worst one.

17

WINNIE

PETER PAN DROPS THE HEART TO THE PATIO AND USES HIS BLOODY hand to grab my arm and yank me away.

I'm still tipsy, but the buzz has burned away, leaving me shivering and foggy.

Pan just killed that boy.

He tore out *his heart.*

Is this really happening?

The others scatter as Pan drags me across the patio and up the stairs. Kas and Bash and Vane follow us.

I try not to trip over my own feet.

When we're back in the house, in the loft, Pan yanks me into the dining room and tosses me into a chair.

He sets his hands on either side of the seat, caging me in.

There is blood splattered across his face and the sight of him covered in carnage makes butterflies take flight in my stomach.

"What part of this do you not understand, Darling?" His

voice is a razor teasing at my skin. One wrong move and the blade will part me, let the blood well to the light.

"Pan," Bash starts, but Pan cuts his gaze to Bash, silencing him.

"I have rules," Pan says.

"So I've heard."

"It's for your safety."

"Is it? Because last I checked, you kidnapped me."

His jaw flexes and he grinds his teeth together.

"I'm trying to save this fucking island," he says.

"I don't care what you're doing," I hear myself say. "This isn't my home. And I didn't take your fucking shadow."

He scowls, then shoots a glare over my head. "Who told her?"

"Wasn't us," Kas says.

"Don't look at me," Vane says. And then, "Probably Cherry."

"You going to kill her too?" I throw in his face. "Maybe you'll kill me next? Dig out my insides and search for your answers. Maybe it's printed here on my bones." I lift my middle finger to him and glare.

He's silent and stoic for a second and then suddenly he's yanking me back to my feet and pressing me to the edge of the table. "What are you doing? What is your plan? Fuck every Lost Boy on the island just to provoke me?"

I frown up at him, catching on the words he used.

There is always something to glean from words, which ones, how they're said.

If they're used as knives or balms.

Provoke me.

Provoke me.

I've gotten to the mighty myth of Peter Pan and my heart beats a little harder with excitement.

"Yes," I hear myself saying. "They call me Winnie Whore, you know. Fucking boys is what I do best."

The breath he takes in is long and labored and it rumbles in the back of his throat.

I tremble beneath him, not from the cold. Never from the cold.

I sense the rising fury in his body, the tremor before the earthquake.

I have one second to breathe before he's spinning me around and bending me over the table.

His left hand presses at the back of my head, driving my face to the wooden table. His other hand bunches my skirt around my waist and yanks down my panties.

I gasp out, sending a fallen leaf skittering over the table.

"If you want to fuck the Lost Boys," Peter Pan says, "why not start at the top?"

He kicks my legs apart, baring me and I hear the rasp of a zipper opening.

"Maybe I will," I say.

My heart is thudding so hard, I swear I can hear it ramming against the table.

This is insane, all of it is insane, but my pussy is throbbing, my clit pulsing, and I can feel myself growing wetter by the second.

I sense Bash and Kas and Vane beyond us, watching, and that makes the butterflies in my stomach turn to a frenzy.

The head of Pan's cock comes to my opening and I let out a little yelp.

The hand at the back of my head tangles in my hair, slides to the back of my neck.

"If you want to act like a whore," he says as he leans over me, "then I'll treat you like a whore."

He shoves into me.

I gasp out.

One of the twins says, "Fuck me," low and beneath his breath as the table shudders from Pan's thrusts inside of me.

He's big, stretching me wide, and I tense beneath him as he slides in and out, not with speed, but force.

The buzz has worn off and there is only the pulsing need in my pussy now, the urge to be released.

I'm slick beneath him. He's hard as a rock.

A moan escapes my raw throat as the pressure at my clit builds and builds. I wiggle beneath him like a cat in heat trying to get any kind of friction against my swollen nub.

Pan knows exactly what I'm doing.

He reaches around to cup me and then stops, his cock buried inside of me.

I gasp out, choke on the breath.

"Do you want to come, Darling?" he asks, his voice rough at my ear.

"Yes," I say, barely a word at all.

"Beg for it."

"What?"

"Beg for it, Darling."

I squeeze my eyes shut, try to come back to my body. I think my soul has left and is floating off to the stars.

I haven't felt this awake in...ever.

"Please," I say and suck in another breath. "Please can I come?"

His fingers shift against me, finding that swollen heat. I cry out, jolt beneath him.

He goes still again, pulls his cock out a fraction, then pushes forward slowly, teasingly.

I'm practically vibrating against the table.

"Please, Pan. Oh god."

"Go on then," he says. "Come for me while the Lost Boys watch."

Then he swirls two fingers around my clit, pumping into me, and I let go.

I am flying.

Soaring.

White stars blink behind my eyes as all the air rushes out of me and a shrill moan escapes my throat.

My nerves burn with pleasure as the heat cascades through my pussy and I clench around him as he drives in deep.

He grows harder, harder, filling me up and then his hands sink to my hips and he slams into me and growls so loudly it makes me shiver.

He rides through the orgasm, angling up against my inner wall, the head of his cock throbbing as he spills the last of his cum.

When he pulls out of me, I slump against the table, panting.

I think that must be it but then Bash comes around the table, a significant bulge in his pants.

"Can I?" Bash asks.

Peter Pan drops into a chair and nods his consent.

Bash gets behind me, still bent over the table. He's bare for me in seconds and nestles into my heat. "Little Darling whore, such a filthy little mess."

I shiver beneath his words.

"Brother," he says. "Get over here."

Kas hesitates and I lift off the table to look down the length of it at him.

There is something dark in his eyes. A hunger he doesn't want to satiate.

Kas is the nice one, but I don't think he's nice enough to deny what he wants to take.

He gets up, kicks a chair aside and comes to the edge of the table by my face.

"Fuck yeah," Bash says as he pushes into me. "Wrap those pretty little lips around my brother's cock."

Kas doesn't wait. Now that he's made his decision, he's ready to act on it.

He takes a length of my hair, wraps it around his fist and guides my mouth over his length.

He fills me up as Bash starts pumping into me.

My heart races in my ears and thuds heavily in my chest.

Kas fucks my mouth roughly, hitting the back of my throat. I gasp, choking on him, and Bash tightens his grip on my hips. "Take it all, Darling. Be a good girl."

Holy shit.

Fuck, this is hot.

Tears fill my eyes as the twins fill me up, fucking me in both holes, relentlessly, mercilessly.

And as they do, I catch sight of Peter Pan in the shadows, watching me get fucked with a look on his face that I think is satisfaction.

And out of all of it tonight, that is what makes me feel most powerful.

I am so fucking alive.

Bash thrusts harder, faster. Kas pumps into my mouth, groaning deep in his chest.

"You ready to fill her up, brother?" Bash says.

"Fuck yeah, I am," Kas says.

And in some kind of fucked up twin synchronicity, they both come at the same time.

Kas spills down my throat and his cum beads sweetly on my tongue just as Bash slams into me from behind with a low grunt.

I lock eyes with Peter Pan.

His gaze is glinting, his lips wet.

I didn't come again, but it almost feels like I did because my nerves are blinking and my belly alighting.

The boys pull out of me and I stay bent over the table breathing heavily through the tingling aftershocks.

"No one else touches her," Pan says. "Do you understand me?"

Bash is still breathing heavily. "Got it."

Vane's footsteps come around the table. A shiver creeps down my spine as I sense him taking up the space behind me.

Is he going to fuck me too?

Fill me with terror and cum?

Do I want that?

Somehow Vane giving in to me might be more of a victory than Pan giving in.

Vane yanks me upright, turns me around. My ass presses against the edge of the table, digging into my flesh.

There is no hint of emotion on Vane's cruelly gorgeous face and it's impossible to read his thoughts in those mismatched eyes.

"Open up, Darling," he orders.

I don't know where this is going, but no one is stepping in and curiosity gets the better of me.

I part my lips. Vane gets in close and spits in my mouth.

"That's all you'll get from me."

I spit it out, dragging my hand over my mouth. "You asshole!" I pummel him with a fist. But hitting him is like hitting a mountain.

Futile. Stupid.

It's Pan that stops me.

"Vane," he says in a low, rumbling warning. "Don't be a dick."

"Why?" he asks. "When I'm so good at it?"

I scowl at him. He smiles at me, all gleaming teeth.

He got the better of me and I'm burning with the need for revenge.

Out of all the things the boys did to me tonight, it's Vane that managed to get beneath my skin.

Asshole.

"Go on," Pan tells him.

Vane cuts me with one last look before turning and walking away.

"Darling," Pan says and I finally look up at him.

"Don't ever provoke me again."

There's still blood on his hand and it finally registers that he killed someone, then fucked me.

What is happening?

And why the hell do I feel so fucking amazing right now?

Is this part of the madness? Driving me to new heights of pleasure and debauchery?

But no...

They don't fuck Darlings.

Or at least, they didn't before me.

"Sleep with the twins tonight," Pan orders. "Don't let her out of your sight again," he adds.

"Come on." Kas offers me his hand. "How about a shower?"

I look over my shoulder at Peter Pan. His pants are still unbuttoned, but his cock is tucked away. He's disheveled and wild, the myth from the mythical island.

Not boy, not man.

A king.

I don't know where I expected this night to go, but it wasn't here.

I am no longer lost.

I think I might have finally been found.

18

KAS

We take the Darling to her room so she can shower. As the water runs, Bash climbs onto her bed and lies back against the pillows. He flicks his wrist and the ceiling turns to twilight and a shooting star shimmers through the night.

There is a reason we both tend to favor the same illusion. It reminds us of the twilight room at the fae palace.

Some days it hurts just thinking about home.

I drop into the wingback and prop my feet on the windowsill. It's silent on the patio where a dead Lost Boy lays. Someone needs to clean up that mess and it isn't going to be me.

"Why do you think Pan gave in tonight?" I ask.

Bash pulls a length of rope from his pocket and starts tying knots. "I don't know. But I'm glad he did."

The ocean breeze turns crisp as the night grows old. It steals in and dries the sweat still clinging to the back of my neck.

"You think Vane will ever give in to her?"

Bash snorts and pulls each end of the rope taut, creating a clover-like knot. "Spitting in her mouth was a favor. She doesn't want Vane to give in to her. He knew that. It's why he did it."

My cock twitches just thinking about Winnie and her pretty little mouth wrapped around me.

Fuck if she isn't better than anyone I've had. Maybe it's because she was forbidden until tonight. Maybe it's something else entirely.

"We should have been watching her tonight."

"If we had, dear brother, Pan wouldn't have lost his shit, and if he didn't lose his shit, he wouldn't have fucked her trying to teach her a lesson, and if he didn't fuck her—"

"Fine. Christ. I get it."

A new knot appears in his hands. "I want to tie her up and do naughty things to her."

Bash is better with ropes than I am, but I enjoy a girl in knots just as much as he does.

"Not tonight," I tell him.

"No, I suppose she's had enough for tonight."

The shower shuts off. I can hear Winnie toweling off, can smell the heady scent of lavender in the soap Cherry bought for her.

We used her tonight. We are no strangers to using pussy for our own pleasure.

But this is different.

Winnie is different and I don't know why.

With a snap of my fingers, fae magic fills the air and the hardwood floor is suddenly covered with plush forest moss and bioluminescent flowers. The light is fake but it still fills the room with a hazy pink glow.

Bash sits up. "You're spoiling her now."

"I want her to think we can be soft."

"Why? She'll only be disappointed when she realizes we aren't."

19

PETER PAN

THERE IS A WRITHING ENERGY IN MY BODY THAT I CANNOT contain.

Everything is at stake and the Darling wants to play fucking games.

I catch up to Vane out in front of the house. "I'm going to murder something. Care to join me?"

"Obviously."

We head toward town by foot. Vane can fly, I cannot.

It's been so fucking long, I can't even remember what it felt like to take to the air.

Like the sun on my skin.

I am as cold as ice and tethered to the earth and I fucking hate all of it.

I'm so fucking angry all of the time.

"Where are we going?" Vane asks.

"Let's go kill some pirates."

"Twist my arm."

We follow the road from the house as it winds through the forest, then crosses Mysterious River, then finally spills into Darlington Port.

Darlington is my city, founded on my blood and magic.

It sits on the southeast edge of the island on the coast.

"Where to?" Vane asks.

"Pirates are always hanging around the Black Dove."

We pass the harbors where ships come in and out from the other islands. There are a few bars along the docks, but pirates like the inland bar, closer to the borderline of my territory so they can duck out quickly if they have to.

This part of town is low on streetlamps so the darkness is longer, the shadows thicker. Mist hangs in the air, the cooler ocean air hitting the heat of the inner city.

Vane lights a cigarette and takes a long drag. "Fucking Darlings now, are we?"

I knew this was coming. I snap my fingers at him and he hands me the cigarette. "I don't have to explain myself to you."

"No. Of course not. Just break all the rules then, I guess, huh?"

I look over at him. I can only see his black eye and the jagged scar that stretches across it. He never told me how he got the wound and I never asked, but the fact that his shadow has hold of that eye tells me all I need to know.

I take another hit and hand the cigarette back.

"I don't know, Vane. If I'm to die soon, why not give in to it all? Huh?"

"You're not going to die."

A group of drunks passes us on the cobblestones and jeers at us until they catch sight of Vane first.

"Apologies, Dark One." They bow, backtracking. "Apologies to our king," they add when they spot me next.

Dark One. Such a ridiculous name. I don't know who started it but it's impossible to undo.

I've found that on every island in the chain, the one that's claimed the Death Shadow is always called the Dark One.

And on almost all of the islands, it's the one with the Life Shadow that has the title of king.

But all these years later, it feels foreign, that word. Like a language I can no longer speak.

I never quite fit the embodiment of it, anyway. I am more death than life.

Perhaps that's why I lost it in the first place, because it was never really mine.

And if it's no longer mine, then what the fuck am I doing?

What happens to the island if I can't reclaim my shadow?

I suppose the fae could sustain it if given the chance. Even more so if Tilly took her brothers back into the fold.

The fae palace is weak without its princes, but she's too stubborn to admit that.

As the road curves toward the fae territory, Black Dove comes into view. The windows are glowing and revelry spills out into the night.

Vane and I stand in the darkness to scan the bar's interior.

"Two of Hook's men in the back," Vane says and inhales the rest of the cigarette before crushing the ember beneath his boot on the cobblestone.

"Two will do."

I am untethered from caution and decency. Only the violence remains.

Vane pulls open the front door and I walk inside.

It takes the bar less than two seconds to notice who's darkened the doorstep and the place goes decidedly silent.

Peanut shells crack beneath my boots as I make my way through the tables to the back corner where Hook's pirates are deep into two glasses of ale.

"Wandered off from home, did you?" I say.

The big burly one takes in a breath, his shoulders straining against the threadbare material of his shirt. "Just out for a drink is all. We mean no harm."

"Harm is subjective, isn't it, Pan?" Vane paces to the other side of their table. "What you think is harmless, we think is a blatant show of disrespect."

The shorter guy sputters and says, "The ale is better here. But don't tell Hook."

"We won't need to," Vane says.

The burly guy tightens his grip on his glass. "Why's that?"

"Because your severed head will do," I say.

The fighting begins with a pop and a crack.

The burly one goes for Vane. Maybe he thinks he has a better chance of taking the Dark One.

Vane punches the guy in the throat, cracking his windpipe and the guy chokes for air.

The shorter one trembles in his chair. I grab him by the collar of his shirt and lift him off the ground. His feet pedal uselessly at the air.

"Sorry, Pan! I'm sorry! It really was just the beer!"

Vane kicks the big guy and more bones crack and as blood taints the air, the Dark One comes out, black eyes glinting in the flickering light of the tavern lanterns.

"Too many rules have already been broken tonight," I tell the guy dangling from my grip. "You just have the bad luck of being on the wrong end of my growing impatience."

Then I slam him to the table and a bone pops out of his arm.

20

WINNIE

I'VE NEVER SLEPT IN A BED WITH SOMEONE ELSE, BUT AS I CLIMB IN beneath the sheets with Kas on my left and Bash on my right, I feel oddly content.

It's like sleeping between two ridiculously hot sentinels.

One of them has created an illusion on the ceiling and another on the floor so that it feels like I'm nestled in a magical forest grove. Pretty little pink flowers glow in the dark.

I am so happy and I don't know why and I don't know what to do with it.

It's a sensation that fits like a coat that's too small, like I might burst the seams if I stretch too far.

I snuggle into Bash's side. He's shirtless and the hazy pink glow lights him up in technicolor. "What's that?" I ask and nod at whatever he has in his hands.

He winds his arm around me and holds up my arm,

tying a rope bracelet around my wrist. There's an acorn cap threaded through the rope.

"A kiss," he says.

"What?"

He laughs through his nose. "The acorn cap is a kiss. It's a thing here. Just pretend it is."

"Okay."

Kas lies on his back, the long line of his body close to mine, our legs touching.

A star darts across the ceiling, leaving a trail of glittering light.

"Two days ago, I thought I was going to go mad," I say, twisting the bracelet around my wrist, admiring the knot work. "Even though Pan kidnapped me, this is somehow better."

Kas snorts. Bash laughs, the deep treble sounding through his chest.

"You might take that back," Bash says.

"Why?"

He sighs. "Go to sleep, Darling."

"I'm not tired."

Crickets chirp beyond the window and there's the soft warble of birds in the tree just beyond my room.

Kas shifts closer and hits a sensitive part of my back and I hiss in response.

"What is it?" he asks.

"It's nothing. I'm fine."

"Did we hurt you?"

"No." I laugh. "You did the opposite. I'm fine, really."

In fact, there's something about Neverland and these Lost Boys that has made the pain fade.

Over the years, I'd gotten use to the constant ache in my

body, the pounding headaches, the sharp, sudden bursts of pain in my nerves.

When you're carved up by witches and so-called voodoo priests, pain becomes second nature. I would take the pain over losing my mind any day, so I never complained. I did what my mother told me to with the slimiest hope that I wouldn't turn out like her.

Thinking about all of this brings some of the memories back and it makes my stomach dip. I know what she did to me was wrong and if I look too closely at it, it makes me want to breakdown and sob.

So I don't.

I don't want to look at it at all.

Your mother is supposed to protect you, but it was my mother's desperate need to save me that caused me the most pain and anguish.

Her love was hard to take some days.

I rest my hand on Bash's flat stomach and close my eyes as Kas twirls a length of my hair around his finger at my back.

I start to drift off even though I didn't think I was tired.

I guess getting fucked by Peter Pan and the Lost Boys is exhausting.

"Darling?" Bash says.

I'm barely awake. "Hmmm?"

"What's your favorite food?"

The question floats around in my head, shrouded in the haziness of sleep.

It takes a lot of effort to decide and even more to get the answer out.

"Croissants."

He laughs lightly. "Really?"

I'm drifting further. The bed is so much more comfortable than my inflatable mattress and Bash is warm at my front and Kas at my back and before I know it, I'm out.

21

WINNIE

WHEN I WAKE THE NEXT MORNING, I'M ALONE IN MY BED AND rain is pattering outside the open windows. The air smells crisp and clean, but there's a considerable chill and I'm only wearing a borrowed t-shirt of Kas's. I certainly didn't pack for a kidnapping.

But when I get up from the bed, I find a thick sweater draped over the wingback chair. I quickly pull it on and drown in it.

I pad out to the kitchen.

Bash is there pouring fresh coffee into a cup. On the counter beside him is a basket of pastries, specifically golden-brown croissants.

I choke on a little sob.

"What's wrong?" he asks, a little amused by my reaction.

It's only now that I remember him asking me my favorite food.

And then he got up early to make it for me?

"Thank you," I say.

"Don't mention it, Darling. After the way your pussy treated me last night, it's the least I can do."

For some reason, it's not the act that made me blush but the reminder of it in the daylight.

Will we ever do that again? All of us?

I want to. I want to very badly and just the thought of it happening again has my nipples pebbling beneath my borrowed clothes and a thrill sinking between my thighs. I haven't had sex like that in, well, ever, and I've had a lot of sex in a very short amount of time, all things considered.

I sit on one of the stools and Bash slides a plate over with a croissant on top of it and the coffee next. The steam kisses my face, wakes me up a bit. "Where is everyone?"

"Kas is out fishing. Vane is...well, who the hell knows where he disappears to. Pan is in his tomb, as usual."

"Why do you keep referring to it as a tomb?" I bring the coffee up to my mouth and blow across it, swirling the steam.

"Because it's literally below ground and has no windows, only one door."

Just like my special room in our crumbling Victorian. Perhaps I have more in common with Peter Pan than I first thought.

"Why does he sleep down there?"

Bash hitches his thumb over his shoulder to the row of windows at his back. "Sunlight kills him."

"What? Really?"

"Yes."

"Why? How?"

"Long story."

"I have time."

"Eat your food, Darling." He's distracted now, his attention wandering to the balcony.

Kas appears a second later. His hair is down and hangs around his shoulders sopping wet. Rain drips from the end of his nose. He's shirtless, because of course he is. These boys do not like shirts. His abs are tight and there is a deep, hollowed groove at his hip bones that sinks down below the waistband of his shorts.

A fresh wave of heat fills me up when I catch myself ogling his crotch. And when I dart my gaze back up to his face, I find him watching me watch him.

The look that comes across his face is dark and carnal.

I shiver and clutch harder at the coffee mug.

"Damn," Bash says and nods at the fish hanging from a rope in Kas's grip. "Been a while since fishing has been that good." Bash takes the rope from his brother and then tosses the fish into the sink. Several of them flap their tails and fish slime arcs through the air.

"Gross." I shove my plate further down the counter, away from the mess.

"What's wrong?" Kas says. "You've never seen dying fish before?"

"Um, no."

The twins look at each other. Bells chime, I swear, though I see no bells.

I may not have known them long, but already I can recognize what those expressions mean—twin mischief.

Kas snaps his fingers at his brother. "Excellent idea."

"Wait, what idea?" I didn't hear any idea.

"We'll teach you how to clean fish," Bash says.

"No." I shake my head for good measure. "I don't want to and have no reason to learn."

"Sure you do." Bash grins at me.

"What's the reason?"

"Fun," he answers.

"Ugh."

"Finish up," he says as another fish flops in the sink. "We have work to do."

Apparently, there's no getting out of this because as soon as I swallow down my last bite of buttery, flaky, oh-so-delicious croissant, Bash is yanking me around the counter.

"Do I really have to do this?" I'm whining a little and I don't even care.

"We are your charming captors," Bash says and smiles. "How can you deny us?"

I frown at him and fold my arms over my middle.

"Here, Darling," Kas says and hands me what looks like a metal brush. He flops a fish onto a thick wooden cutting board. Thankfully, this fish is dead and doesn't jump around. "Hold it by the tail," he says and shows me how, "then rake the fish scaler over it from the tail to the head. Like this." He drags the brush over the fish's body and scales come off in clumps, but several fly off too and one lands smack dab on my face.

My mouth screws up as the overwhelming scent of fish fills my nose.

Laughing, Kas reaches over, plucking the scale from my cheek.

"Already a natural," he says.

"Is this like a normal day for you two?" I ask and resume the scaling.

"Fishing on an island? Making messes? Yes." Bash pulls

himself up on the counter opposite me. "Some days are saved for taking care of naughty Darlings though."

I shoot him a glare. He winks at me.

"I don't need to be taken care of." I reposition the fish to get around one of the fins. More scales fly through the air.

"I disagree." Kas's voice is light, but his gaze dark.

My face pinks again. "I've literally taken care of myself my entire life on my own. When my mom wasn't out escorting old white men, she was home descending further and further into madness. The only person I could count on was me."

"Old white men, eh?" Bash says behind me.

"You know the ones."

"Of course I do. There are a dozen buried beneath this house. We enjoyed breaking them."

"You're joking." I look at Kas. "Is he joking?"

Kas shakes his head.

"Why?"

"I think the better question is, why not?" Bash says.

"Do you all just go around murdering on the regular?"

"Yes," Bash answers. "We murder a lot."

"Why?"

"Because in this world, and in yours, if you're not the monster, then you're the prey. And we can't have that, Darling. Especially when it comes to old white men." He laughs like it's a joke but I know he's not kidding.

"Flip over," Kas says.

"What?" I blink up at him.

"The fish. Flip it over and scale the other side."

"Right." I do as he asks and when I'm done, he orders me to step aside. He pulls out a sharp knife and runs it over a block of stone, sharpening it. The quick movements make a rasping sound.

"Are you watching?" he asks.

"Yes."

"Insert the blade here." He points the tip just below the fish's mouth. "Then run it back to the anal fin."

I blanch at the mention of *anal*.

Why is everything the boys do sexual?

He's quick and precise with his movements and the fish's belly parts beneath his hand. Guts spill out.

"Cut here," he says next and lifts a fin by its head, angling the blade in.

"You're good with a knife," I hear myself saying.

He makes several more cuts and the fish's guts come clean out.

"He's not just good," Bash says. "He's an expert with a blade." He hops off the counter, comes over to me and yanks down the waistband of his pants, revealing an old scar with an intentional design.

It's a circle with several lines through it, then more forks off the lines.

"What is that?"

"Symbol of our house," he answers.

"This house?"

Kas stops cutting and glares at his brother over his shoulder. "Must we dredge this up?"

"He's still salty about it." Bash grabs a croissant from the basket and starts for the door. "I suppose you'll hear it from our sister soon enough, so what's the sense in waiting? We're princes of the fae."

22

KAS

I can feel the Darling look at me with new interest.

This is precisely why I don't like telling the Darlings who we are and especially not this one.

Being a prince makes people treat you differently. Even if you are sullied.

"Is that true?" she asks low.

"It is." I finish filleting the fish in hand then toss the spine and the ribs into a bowl, the filet into another.

"If you're princes, then why are you here?"

"We were banished."

"Why?"

I start gutting a second fish. "Are you sure you want to know?"

"Yes."

"Kas and I killed our father."

The admission steals some of the oxygen from my lungs.

The memory is still vivid all of these years later. The

anger that came over his face when the blade sunk deep. Followed by shock when he realized he was going to die from the wound.

It took all of ten seconds.

One minute our father was alive and the next he was on the floor, rimmed in blood.

"Why?" she asks again.

"Because we could."

Not the real reason, but the real reason is more complicated and I've dredged up too much already.

If it wasn't for the blade in my hand, I might be losing my damn mind.

I understand Winnie's fear of going mad. I worry about it every single fucking day.

If I go mad, it will be karma driving it.

I finish cleaning the fish in silence and the Darling watches me intently.

"Is that for dinner?"

"No," I answer. "It's payment."

"For what?"

I finally look up at her. Her hair is shiny and soft after her shower. It makes me want to rub blood through it, dirty her up.

The rain is pouring outside the windows now and everything feels farther away.

"For my sister."

Tonight Tilly will come to see the Darling now that the moon is full.

It's been decades since I saw her last.

I miss her more than I thought I could. More than I thought I would.

It was always Bash and me protecting her and now who does she have in that vast palace on the other side of the island? Our court had always been conniving and duplicitous.

I hate the thought of my little sister being there alone without champions.

We were supposed to be her knights, princes of the fae.

Instead, we are erased.

23

WINNIE

I don't know what to expect with Bash and Kas's sister. Will she have wings like her brothers did?

And if they're princes, then what is she?

I'm beginning to learn that nothing is as it seems here.

After the fish cleaning, I spend the rest of the day exploring the loft. There's the living room, the hallway to the bedrooms, with mine at the end and the twins' across the hall.

There's a second hall off the living room that leads to the other side of the house.

Here I find another bathroom, another spare bedroom, and a library. There is a giant circular window that overlooks the ocean and rain patters softly against the glass.

And sitting in a leather chair beneath it, boots propped up on a coffee table, is Vane.

I'm already over the threshold before I spot him, so I come to a halt, turn away, then decide, *no*, I'm not going to run away. Didn't he tell me not to run away?

There's a book in his hands with a black cloth cover and a title stamped in gold. I'm too far away to make out what it says.

When I come in, for a split second, his good eye zeroes in on me then narrows, before turning back to the page.

He resumes reading, pretending I'm not there at all.

"What are you reading?" I ask.

"None of your business," he answers easily.

I come closer so I can read the title. "Frankenstein. How fitting."

He lays the open book on his chest. "Did you want something?"

I shrug and clasp my hands behind my back suddenly feeling like a kid that's been let out in a zoo. I want to press my face against the glass and peer in at all the wild beasts.

"Why are you such a jerk?" I ask and drop into the chair across from him.

"It comes naturally." He smiles tightly at me with white teeth and sharp incisors.

It's hard to look directly at him without immediately gaping at the scar and the black eye. It's like a monster is trying to claw its way out of his face.

"Is it because you possess the shadow of death?"

He goes still, eyes glinting in the gloomy light.

"And what does the little girl know of the shadow of death?"

I get the first creeping sense of dread and try to act casual as I consider his question. "Not much. Just that it makes you a raving lunatic."

He snaps the book shut and sets it on the table. "And what does that make you, entering a room alone with me? A glutton for punishment?"

Fuck. Just the mere suggestion that he might do something to me, bend me over his knee, fuck me against the wall, has me clenching. I squeeze my thighs together trying to ward off the tingle spreading between my legs.

Of course he notices me squirming. His tongue pokes at the inside of his cheek.

I am out of my depth here.

"Maybe it does," I admit because I suspect I can't keep anything from Vane. If only I could read him as easily as he can read me.

"You should get up out of that chair and walk right back out that door."

"Why?"

He inhales, slow and deep.

Last night when he spit in my mouth, I wanted to tear him apart. Out of all the idiots I've slept with, none have ever treated me like a slut even though I sorta was. I'm not ashamed of my life choices. For the last decade, I was expecting my life to end on my 18th birthday. Maybe not literally, but figuratively. A slow descent into madness.

So I took what I wanted, how I wanted it, because none of it felt like it mattered anyway.

Even though my 18th birthday has come and gone, and now that I'm in Neverland and the myth of Peter Pan has proven itself to be real, I still can't shake the feeling like I'm running on borrowed time.

And if I am, I want to continue to *take*.

I want to do whatever the fuck I want even if it kills me.

So I get up out of that chair, but instead of walking out the door, I cross the distance between me and Vane and climb on his lap.

He growls, but his hips shift, lining himself up at my center. I don't know if it's on purpose or base instinct.

He keeps his arms on the chair as he turns up to me.

"Now that you're here," he says, "what do you plan to do about it?"

He's tempting me, teasing me. He shifts again, this time pressing forward with his hips. He's not hard yet though, and it pisses me off.

All of those needy, inexperienced football players were hard on a dime.

But...he's got a good point.

What do I plan to do? My plan had no end point. Just a beginning.

I can't turn back now. I'll look like a coward and he'll be gratified with the fact that I couldn't follow through with my recklessness.

So I do the only thing a girl can do in this scenario—I pull off my sweater and my t-shirt.

I'm not wearing a bra so my breasts hit the air and my nipples immediately shrink to dark beads.

Vane growls again and now, *now* he's hard.

I am full of so much pride I might float off into the rain cloud.

Just as long as he doesn't see my back, just as long as he doesn't see my scars.

I don't want him to think me weak.

His hands come to my hips and he grinds me down on him.

The air gets stuck in my throat.

"Pretty little Darling whore," he says. "Trying to pretend she's bigger than she is."

"Vicious shadow of death," I say, "trying to pretend like this is all beneath him."

"I made no such claim." His hand trails from my hip, up my waist, and a shiver rocks over my shoulders. My nipples are so tight now, they're painful and desperate for warmth.

Vane sits forward and brings his mouth to my peak.

I inhale in a hiss as he slides his tongue over me, then bites at me.

He wraps his arm around my waist, rocking me against him.

This is happening.

I'll have them all when this is over.

I rub my pussy against his shaft, wishing there was no clothing between us. Do I make the first move or does he?

Take, that voice says in the back of my mind.

Take what you want.

I reach down between us and start to unbutton his pants. I'm trembling from anticipation and fear.

At any moment, he could turn that dark power on me, the terror.

His mouth still on my nipple, he turns up to me.

"Look at me," he orders.

His dark hair hangs over his forehead and his violet eye is bright.

The air gets lodged in my throat as the terror slithers in and his face turns sharp.

Before I know what's happening, he has me pinned on the floor, his entire body vibrating with barely restrained rage.

"Listen to me very carefully, Darling." His teeth grind together. "You do not want to fuck with me."

I choke down air, trying to keep the terror at bay as my heart pounds a warning in my ears. "I just want to be fucked *by* you."

He sits up and slaps my tit.

I jolt, yelping in shock, and he clamps his hand over my mouth and the terror swells to a crescendo in my gut.

Every fiber in my body is telling me to get up and run.

It's a crawling sensation beneath my skin that I can't shake.

Run far. Run fast.

Run. Run.

RUN.

Hand still clamped over my mouth, he says, "*No.*"

One menacing word delivered with enough fire to burn.

My body is writhing for something, anything. Release or defeat or pain or pleasure.

I can't contain it and I can't think straight and my clit is throbbing.

"Please," I say, the word muffled around his hand.

The pressure of his body is gone in a beat and I blink up at the loss of him.

"I'm not going to make you my pretty little broken fuck doll," he tells me, and then he stalks from the room and I gulp down air.

I lie there on the rug for several long minutes, not entirely sure what just happened and if I actually survived it.

Am I dead?

I feel like I just leapt off of a cliff, but I haven't hit yet. I'm still falling.

As the dark clouds roll in and the rain falls harder, I finally breathe normally and crawl up to my knees to fetch my sweater.

I get dressed and collapse into Vane's abandoned chair, feeling spent but unsatisfied too.

Goddamn him.

I hate him. Which just makes me want to make him give in even more. Just so I can gloat about it.

But maybe he's right—wanting that might make me a glutton for punishment.

And oh how sinister that punishment would be.

24

PETER PAN

WHEN I COME UP FROM THE TOMB, I FIND THE DARLING IN THE library curled in one of the leather chairs by the giant circular window. She's just staring at the glass as rain plinks against it, but there's a book open in her hands.

The sun is gone, but it's hard to know for sure, the sky is so heavy and dark.

She is a tempting sight. Like a wild, exotic bird that I want to capture and cage so that only I can hear her sing.

When she realizes I'm there, she blinks over at me and shifts in the chair, unfolding her legs from beneath her. She's wearing only an oversized sweater, her legs bare. I could easily slip my hand up her thighs, steal in beneath the sweater, make her writhe beneath me.

I get a flash of what I did to her last night and my cock aches for a repeat. I don't get lost in pussy that often. Sometimes I need to fuck just to feel, but I haven't fucked like that in a long time.

"Hi," she says to me.

It's such a simple word, casual and light. A mortal word.

No one says hi to me. Hi is for friends and I have no friends.

Only enemies and allies.

And even the latter feels hollow and thin lately.

"Hi."

She smiles at me, pretty little Darling girl. I want to drive her to the floor and shove my dick in her mouth, watch her gag on it.

I am not a nice man. I am a worse king.

I can pretend though, for now.

"What are you reading?"

She shuts the book and looks down at it, as if only just now realizing she had it. "Frankenstein."

"Classic."

"I guess."

She's reading a book about monsters in a den of monsters.

How fucking poetic.

"I need to prepare you for tonight," I tell her and she looks up with interest. I don't usually warn the Darlings of what's to come. I don't know why I feel the need to warn *her*.

"Okay."

"My shadow," I say. "It was a Darling that took it."

She frowns. "Which one?"

"It was a very long time ago. Several generations back."

I can't speak her name because I have forgotten it.

There is only a dark void where she used to exist and all that remains is the feeling of her.

"Memories of your ancestors can be inherited," I tell her. "Buried in blood. But memories are wild and tumultuous in children. That's why..." I trail off, sighing.

"That's why you take the Darlings at eighteen," she guesses.

"Yes."

"How do you search the memories?"

"The fae can get inside a mind, but especially the queen."

Her tongue flicks out and wets her lips. "That's why they all go mad, isn't it?" Her eyes well up and I have to fight the urge to reassure her.

It'd be a fucking lie, anyway. It's the truth. When Tilly comes, by the end of the night, the Darlings are changed.

So then I bide my time, waiting for the next generation to come of age, waiting for this moment.

But now... I don't want this Darling to change.

Usually when I take them, they rave and scream, or they sob and quiver.

This one is like a feral cat that wants to push the saucer of milk off the table just to watch it spill.

I like that about her.

Brave little Darling girl. Wild and reckless, always up for depraved adventure.

"Is there any way to get to the memories without risking the insanity?" she asks.

I lean back into the chair. "I wouldn't know. That's not my area of specialty."

"So what is?"

Good question. I don't seem to have one anymore. I used to have many. I could fly, for one. I could look beyond myself, into the island and just know things about it. I could make anything appear out of thin air. Food or animal or trinkets or treasure. If I thought it, I could create it.

I haven't been able to do any of that in a very long time.

Now the bushes don't produce the same number of

berries, and the coconut trees produce fewer coconuts and the bays are yielding fewer catches. The weather shifts more than it used to.

I claimed the shadow of life a very long time ago and it was my responsibility to keep it.

And without it, the island is dying.

I am dying.

"I don't want to go mad," the Darling says.

Her voice catches and her eyes fill with tears.

She can go toe to toe with the Dark One but facing the loss of her sanity is the thing that terrifies her the most.

I think perhaps we have more in common, this Darling and I.

"Get dressed," I tell her.

"Why?" She's immediately on guard.

"Let me take you for a walk and show you something."

She narrows her eyes at me.

"You will be safe," I tell her. "From me and the island. I assure you."

"All right. I could stretch my legs."

She sets the book aside and passes me and I have to fight the urge to reach out and snatch her. This is why we never touched the Darlings. Once you've got a taste, it's hard to forget the flavor.

She goes to her room and I go to the loft to pour a drink.

I'm not as tired as I was yesterday, but my fucking head is pounding.

I sling back a shot of whisky, then light a cigarette, letting the smoke ache in my lungs.

I don't know where everyone is and I don't fucking care.

When the Darling comes back, she's wearing her dress and that sweater that hangs off her bony shoulders, and something stirs in my gut at the sight of her, so tiny and fragile.

I can't breathe.

"Lead the way," she says.

There are many paths that lead from the house into the island's forest. The forest is what stands between us, Darlington Port, and the fae territory.

The rain has let up to a breezy mist that coats my skin.

I take the Darling on the path that heads north into the heart of the forest. She's silent beside me but it's hard not to notice the loudness of her presence.

"Where did you get your scars?" I ask her.

She inhales sharply, keeps her eyes on the path.

"Darling."

"A hazard of being a Darling, I suppose." She tries to smile up at me, but it's forced.

"Who did them?"

The thought of someone carving her flesh makes me angrier than it should. I shouldn't fucking care. I don't care.

Yes, you fucking do.

"People my mother hired." She grabs a firecracker flower from a listing bush and starts plucking petals from the stem, leaving them behind us like bright red breadcrumbs. "She was trying to protect me."

"She had an odd way of showing it."

Darling rubs a petal between her thumb and forefinger, then brings it to her nose, inhaling the sharper floral scent now that the oils have broken through to her skin.

"It was because of you," she says, her voice edged in

accusation. "If you didn't kidnap Darlings, I might have had a normal life."

Guilt burrows into me.

But I am nothing if not fair. I only give what I get.

"If the Darling hadn't stolen my shadow, I wouldn't have to steal Darlings."

She frowns over at me. "I guess that's true." She tosses the naked flower stem into the brush. "How did she steal it anyway? My ancestor?"

Just thinking about it makes my skin crawl.

"There was a coup," I tell her and that will be all I tell her.

"Who?"

Those are skeletons I don't want to unbury.

Thankfully, I don't have to. We've arrived at our destination. "Look." I pull back an overgrown fern to reveal the Never Lagoon.

The Darling stops on the path, her mouth agape, her eyes wide. "Whoa."

White sand surrounds the lagoon and the water that fills it is bright turquoise, even beneath the gloomy sky.

It butts up against Marooner's Rock so that the lagoon is mostly hidden, nestled between rock and forest.

Rain continues to patter against the leaves. "Come closer," I tell her and take her hand, and she inhales at my touch.

My chest tightens.

We go to the water's edge.

"Look down," I tell her.

There is no great depth to the lagoon, but it's full of magic. Or it was once, and so when you look straight down, it's like looking through a portal.

And in that swirl of water and magic, glowing shapes swim back and forth almost like a slow-motion dance.

Every now and then a face turns to the surface, eyes glowing bright.

"Holy shit," the Darling says and staggers back. I catch her before she stumbles over her feet.

I can't help but laugh. The sound of it catches me off guard.

"What are those?" she asks. "They look like mermaids or ghosts."

"Maybe a little of both."

Tink once told me the lagoon was a portal to the afterlife, that the shapes swimming beneath the surface were trapped souls.

I skirt the shore and pluck a stone from the sand and send it skipping over the water. Swirls of light rise up to meet it.

"This is...amazing," the Darling says.

"Your mother said the same thing."

She frowns. "You brought my mom here?"

"She was...not well," I admit. "Sometimes the lagoon can be healing. I thought maybe it would help her."

The girl is looking at me now like she doesn't recognize me.

"You tried to help her?"

She softens and takes a step toward me.

I turn away. "She was sobbing all night long," I say. "Had to shut her up somehow."

That's not true. Not entirely. Merry had been sobbing, but for a much different reason.

And when she told me—

I pluck another stone from the sand but this time when

I toss it, it sails clean across the lagoon and lets out a resounding crack when it hits the face of Marooner's Rock.

"Did it help her?" Darling asks. "The lagoon?"

The rain picks up again and when I turn back to the Darling, she's trembling in the cold.

My chest catches on a growl. I take off my shirt in one quick yank of fabric and go to her. "Arms up, Darling," I order and she dutifully follows my command. It's not a thick shirt, but it'll do for now.

"Tell me," she says and peers up at me. Mist clings to her lashes and rain drips from the end of her nose. "Please."

I sigh. "I think so, for a while anyway."

She nods. "Thank you."

"Don't thank me," I say. "The reason she was in need of anything was because of me. Remember?"

She frowns at me, her gaze searching for things that I don't think I possess but desperately want to give her.

"Come. Tilly will be to the house soon. We best get back."

She needs warm, dry clothes. That's what she needs.

It's the least I can give her before the fae queen digs into her head.

25

WINNIE

Peter Pan's shirt smells like him. Like wild forest and heady nights.

I pull it closer to my torso to keep in some of my body heat while I follow him back through the woods.

When we emerge and the house comes into view, I pause for a second. It's the first I've really looked at the house from the front. It's massive, hugged on both sides by wild, tropical forest. Bright flowers dot the surrounding trees and several palms rise high above. All of the windows of the house are lit up, sending a golden glow into the descending night.

My mom said there was magic on the island. The illusions the twins cast were certainly magic, but now I know what my mom was really talking about. The lagoon, the swimming souls that looked like mermaids, and the house glowing with life.

I love it here, even though that feels like a leap considering I've barely been here at all.

There's something about it that feels familiar, that feels like returning home after a long trip. A place to sigh with contentment.

I've never had that. Never in my entire life.

I follow Pan up the steps to the balcony and then into the loft. The giant tree in the center of the house is full of little fireflies.

"There you are," Vane says. "Where the fuck have you been?"

Pan grumbles at him. "Out."

Vane eyes me with his glittering violet eye. I can't tell what he's thinking and I'm usually so good at reading people. Maybe that's why he's so damn frustrating. I can't get beyond his walls and see inside.

He is a puzzle box and I want to find the solution to break him open.

The twins come into the room. "Tilly is on her way."

Peter Pan snaps his fingers at Vane. "Get the rest of the Lost Boys into the house and out of sight. Bash and Kas, get the Darling some dry clothes and help get her ready."

My heart leaps to my throat and blood rushes to my head, pounding against my ears. This is it. This is how it happens.

I don't want to lose my mind.

"Darling?" Kas stops in front of me. His hair is tied back again in a bun at the back of his head. There's worry in his amber eyes.

"I don't want to do this."

He frowns at me. "The king gets what he wants."

I gulp down air. "Please, Kas."

He slips his arm around my shoulders and guides me toward the bedroom.

I'm shaking and numb.

This is how it happens. This is when it begins.

"Why does she have to get into my head? Can't I just be like hypnotized or something? Don't you think that if any of us knew where it was, we would have remembered by now? Please, Kas." I grab his hands, squeeze.

"I can't stop it, Win," he says and tilts his head. "And you can't either."

Bash comes into the room. "Listen, Darling. You may be at risk of being knocked over by a stiff breeze, but in here"—he ruffles my hair—"you're stronger than you think. And you're going to let our dear sister get into your head and you're going to help us find Peter Pan's shadow. Okay? I believe that. I believe you're different from every single Darling that's come before you."

I swallow against the lump growing in my throat. "You think so?"

"Yeah." He grins at me. "We got to fuck you."

Kas whacks him upside the back of the head and then Bash reaches over and does the same to his twin.

I want to help Pan.

I want to be the one that gets him his shadow.

But I don't want to lose my head doing it.

I have endured. I've endured the sickness of so-called magic potions that only made me vomit for days. I've endured blades cutting into my flesh, the blood collected to paint across my ceiling.

I have endured and I can endure this.

I can finally end this curse for all of us.

"Okay." I nod and pull Peter Pan's shirt off. "I can do this."

"That's right," Kas says. "I'll go see if Cherry has some clean, dry clothes somewhere."

When Kas is gone, Bash comes over to me and takes my

hand in his. He fingers the bracelet around my wrist, spins it around my arm. "This isn't just a regular bracelet."

"I know. It's a kiss."

"Yes, but there's more." He smiles down at me, voice raspy and low as he continues. "It's imbued with magic. It'll protect you. You have nothing to fear."

I know he has magic. Maybe he's telling the truth.

I give him a nod.

Unlike my mother and her mother and her mother's mother, I can come out the other side of this intact.

It's going to be all right.

Cherry lends me a clean dress, but it sags on my shoulders so I fuss over it constantly so that my back isn't bared.

"Darling," Pan calls.

I come out to the loft where he, the twins, and Vane are waiting. The rest of the house is silent.

"Are you ready?" Pan asks.

"I think so."

There is the distinct sound of horse hooves on the cobblestones outside the house.

Bash goes to the window. "She's here."

Even though I'm the one who's supposed to be subjected to mental torture, I sense the twins' shifting energy. They're nervous to see their sister.

As we wait for them to come up to the loft, I try not to fidget but fail. I am a ball of nerves too.

Their sister is a queen. A fae.

I'm excited to meet her because of that but dreading what she's here to do.

When she comes up the stairs to the loft, I hold my breath.

And when she finally appears, I can't help but gasp.

She's like a fairy straight out of a fairytale.

And she has wings. Large gossamer wings that arch from her back and flutter slowly beneath the light of the glowing lanterns. And when they catch the right lighting, they shimmer like the inside of an abalone shell.

Her dark hair is braided into several braids that are woven in and around a delicate golden crown where a single stone glitters in the center.

She has the twins' high, sharp cheekbones and thin, straight nose. But her face is heart-shaped where theirs is more angular.

Turning her gaze on me, I notice her irises are the same shimmery, shifting color of her wings.

She's magnificent.

She's more myth than Peter Pan himself.

I blink several times as if to double check that my vision isn't playing tricks on me.

"Tilly," Peter Pan says and comes over to her. "I'm happy to see you."

She smiles up at him, but some of the light fades from her eyes and it's the first hint that something is amiss between them.

Does Peter Pan know?

She holds out her hand to him, fingers bent. He reaches over, takes her hand and plants a kiss to her knuckles.

That pleases her. Almost like being kissed is a display of dominance and she likes being the dominant one.

I suppose Peter Pan is at her mercy. She's the only one who can dig inside my head.

Then she turns her gaze on the twins flanking me and all of the pleasure bleeds from her face.

Now her expression is cold and distant.

"Brothers," she says.

"Dear sister," Bash says.

"It's nice to see you, Tilly," Kas says.

She doesn't respond and I can tell the short conversation leaves both of the twins wanting.

"Is this the Darling?" she asks and cuts her gaze to me.

It's hard not to turn my face to the floor like a cowering idiot.

"Hi."

"Have these feral boys minded their manners?"

Vane snorts.

I try to ignore him. "Yes. They've been kind."

Except for when they were calling me a whore and fucking me over the table.

I'd take that over this any day.

In fact, I'd prefer it over just about anything else.

I want to go back to that, when the only pursuit was my own pleasure.

"Come, have a seat." She gestures to one of the chairs and I reluctantly make my way across the room to it and sit down.

I fold my hands into my lap to hide my trembling fingers. My skin is clammy and my knee is bouncing.

"This shouldn't take more than a few minutes," she says behind me and a creeping sense of dread crawls over my shoulders.

My heart is racing and my stomach is knotted up and I think I could vomit if given a bucket to do it in.

Tilly reaches out for my head and I flinch.

"It's okay. I'm just putting my hands here." Her fingers

sink into the threads of my hair so that they can press directly to my scalp. "Ready?"

God no. Not at all.

What if there is no memory of the stolen shadow? What if all of this is for nothing and all of the Darling women have had their brains scrambled for nothing more than a wild goose chase?

"Let's begin," she says and blinding pain cracks through my skull.

26

BASH

My sister won't even look at us. We are royalty and yet she regards us like we are serfs from the berry fields.

Everything Kas and I did, we did for her.

Kas wants to be forgiven, but I'm beginning to crave revenge.

Our sister's jeweled fingers thread their way through Winnie's hair. An overwhelming sense of urgency wells up my throat.

I've seen this done many times before. I know how this ends.

"Let's begin," our sister says.

Bright white light glows beneath her hands and Winnie's face contorts with pain.

Beside me, Kas shifts his weight from one foot to the other like he's fighting the urge to leap across the room and take our dear sister down.

Winnie screams.

Pan grits his teeth.

The light builds as our sister digs in and roots around inside the Darling's head.

Does she even know what she's looking for all of these years later? Does she care enough to dig deep enough?

All at the expense of our little Darling.

Tilly focuses in on the task, fingers turning into claws as she shoves forward with her power.

Kas and I once watched her turn a man's brains into mush because he insulted her in front of the court. She put her hands to his head and ten seconds later, his brain was leaking out his nose.

I shouldn't care about what happens to Winnie, but the gnawing of my conscience is making it difficult.

I don't want her to turn out like the rest—dazed and faraway.

Like her mother. We made Merry a promise and we broke it.

There is a single moment where I consider stopping Tilly, damn the consequences.

I nearly do it too.

But someone else beats me to it.

Not my brother. Not Pan.

But Vane.

It's the Death Shadow that leaps in.

27

WINNIE

THE PAIN SINKS DEEP. IT IS WORSE THAN THE CONSTANT, DULL ache I've lived with nearly my entire life. Worse than the blades that etched fake magic into my skin.

This pain is all over. It feels like Tilly is touching my soul with claws and fire. Tearing through the very fabric of who I am and what I am.

I can't move, it hurts so bad. There is only the bright white light and the sharp ache.

I try to hold on as best I can.

I can do this, I try to tell myself.

I have endured.

But I can't.

I can't do it.

I want it to stop.

I want to seep away like a river, disappear over the horizon.

Just let go.

Peter Pan needs you.

The Lost Boys needs you.

The island needs you.

None of this is mine, but yet I feel I have a duty to save it.

Endure. Endure.

Just a little longer.

I can't be sure, but I think I start shaking beneath Tilly's hands. I can't feel my legs and my hands are clawed around the arms of the chair.

Hold on.

Endure.

These brutal, vicious boys might have used me in the vilest way possible, but in that moment, I finally felt free.

I felt alive.

There is something about Peter Pan and the Lost Boys that feels like a liberation.

I can do this.

And it's then, when some distant part of me gives in to it, when I decide to endure for them and not because of them, that something clicks into place.

And then the light cuts out and the pain ebbs away and I collapse into Vane's arms.

"No more," he says. His voice is a distant rumble over top of me. I have the distinct sensation of being lifted in the air, cradled against a solid chest.

"Vane." Pan's voice rings with authority.

"No. We're not fucking doing this anymore." Vane starts away.

"I wasn't done," Tilly calls.

"I'm saying you're done." He keeps walking, his footsteps heavy on the hardwood floor.

"Where are you taking her?" A beat, then, "Vane, for Christ's sake."

A door opens, then slams shut. A bolt clicks into place.

"Vane!"

"Darling?" Vane's voice is hoarse above me. "You still with me?"

My response is thick and muzzy. "I think so."

He lays me down on a bed. The room is dark and warm and it smells like him, like dark, summer nights and crushed amber.

He starts to pull away but I take a fistful of his shirt. "Don't go."

There is a second where it seems like he'll leave anyway. After all, I think he hates me, which doesn't explain why I'm currently in his bed, why he would defy Peter Pan.

"Move over," he finally tells me and though my body aches, I do as he says.

The bed sinks beneath his weight and then he takes me into his arms, nestles me against him.

My ear at his chest, I hear the steady thrum of his heart.

I've never felt as safe as I do in this moment and I don't know how to feel about that.

It makes me want to sob.

"Why did you do that?" I ask, my voice catching.

"Stop asking questions and just rest," he says.

"Why, Vane?"

His arm comes around me, his fingers sure at my waist. "Because I felt like it, and because I could."

"That's not an answer."

He sighs. "Where I come from, little girls like you are

broken every day for no other reason than to watch them crack. And I'm fucking sick of it."

His breath is warm against my pounding skull.

"I'm stronger than you think," I tell him.

"Even the mighty oak believes she is strong until a man comes along with an ax to chop her down."

"Is that you then? Do you have an ax?"

"All men are born with an ax in their hands, Darling. To take the measure of a man, you just have to pay attention to how he wields it."

I sigh against him.

"Now rest." His hand trails up to my temple and warmth spreads beneath his touch. Within seconds, I'm out.

28

WINNIE

I'M IN A ROOM I DON'T RECOGNIZE, BUT THE WOMAN IN FRONT OF me seems familiar. She's got thick auburn hair pulled back into a barrette.

My great-grandmother Wendy's trunk is in front of us and the woman is holding a box in her hands.

"Who are you?" I ask, but she doesn't hear me and my voice floats around the room like I'm under water.

She ducks down, unlatches the trunk and pushes the lid back. It's lined the same as it is now with creamy paper printed with little orange flowers.

Setting her smaller box aside, she reaches into the trunk, knocks on the side and then a drawer pops open.

"I didn't know that was there."

She scoops up the smaller box, places it into the drawer and presses it closed.

When she stands up, she dusts her hands off like it's a job well done.

"He can never have it back," a voice says behind us.

I turn with the auburn-haired woman as a figure steps out of the shadows.

A woman with gossamer wings and sharp, bright eyes. If the wings weren't shocking enough, the soft, golden glow surrounding her would be. She's lit up almost like a night star.

She looks like Tilly but different.

The auburn-haired woman stands frozen, eyes glossy and far away.

She reminds me of my mother in that way.

The winged-woman steps closer and puts her hand to the woman's head.

The light pulses around the room, blinding me and I turn away from it.

And as I do, I see the face of a child peering out from a closet.

When the light fades away and I look again, the auburn-haired woman is lying on the floor, unmoving, unblinking. Not breathing.

Before the winged woman leaves, she adds, almost under her breath, "And he'll certainly never have his Darling."

🍃

I lurch awake.

The bed is empty and I'm disoriented for a second trying to remember where I am.

"Vane?" I call.

There's no answer.

I throw the sheet back and leave the room. Daylight shines beyond the darkened bedroom. Kas and Bash are in the loft with Vane at the bar.

"Darling," Kas says as he lurches upright to meet me halfway. "How are you feeling?"

"Where is he?"

"Who?"

"Peter Pan."

"It's daytime," Vane says, a little bored. "He's in his tomb."

"Where?"

"In the bottom of the tower."

"Where?"

They just stare at me.

"Fine. I'll find it myself."

I start back the way I came. From the outside of the house, there's only the one tower on the north side so I go there and find a door easily enough.

"You won't get far," Vane says suddenly behind me.

I ignore him, yank the door back and peer down the darkened tower. The shuffling of my feet echoes in the vast, dark space.

"You need a key to get into the tomb," Vane says.

"Then give me the key."

"Why?" He's behind me now, towering over me.

"I need to ask him something."

"What?"

"Come down with me and you'll find out."

"If you wake him in the daytime, he could very well kill you."

I square my shoulders, fold my arms over my chest, and wait him out.

His curiosity gets the better of him. He goes down first and I trail behind him, hand close on the metal banister.

Soft inset lighting keeps me from falling off the winding

stairwell and when we reach the bottom, I shiver at the chill in the air. We're far below ground now.

Vane unlocks the door and pulls it open to reveal an empty annex and a second door.

"After you," he says.

On the second door, I lift up the handle and pull it open.

The room really is a tomb. It's pitch black.

I grope around inside. "Where's the light switch?"

Vane grumbles and edges past me. A second later, a lamp flicks on and golden light spills over the room.

There's a giant four-poster bed in the center of the room, a dresser, a wingback chair and stacks and stacks of what look like leather-bound journals.

The bed is empty.

"Where—"

"What is it?"

His voice slithers out from the shadows. He's barely a shape in a darkened doorway and it reminds me of the first time I laid eyes on him in our old Victorian. Back then I was afraid of what he symbolized.

I'm not afraid anymore.

I cross the room and stop a foot from him.

"Who had glowing skin and wings and looked like Tilly?"

His face darkens. "Why?" There is a noticeable growl in the back of his throat.

"Just tell me."

"Tink," Vane answers. "It was Tinker Bell."

I look at him over his shoulder. "What happened to her?"

"I killed her," Pan says. He sighs and rubs at his eyes. "What is this about? I'm very tired, Darling."

"This is about your shadow."

That gets his attention.

He comes over to the edge of the bed and sits down like standing takes too much effort. He's shirtless, in nothing but loose pajama pants. I'm realizing this is the first time I've seen him unclothed, the first time I'm getting a good look at the tattoos that are inked between the scars.

He's covered in them.

"It might have been a Darling that took my shadow, but it was Tink who masterminded the entire thing with the help of one of the Lost Boys. With Tootles."

"Tootles." What an odd name. "Why would Tink do that?"

"Because Tinker Bell was in love with Peter," Vane answers.

"That makes no sense. If she loved you—"

"She may have loved me," he says, "but she hated Darlings more."

"So?"

"So...I just happened to love one. I was in love with the original Darling."

All of the air is knocked out of my chest and I collapse on the bed beside Pan.

When I decided to barrel down here, I didn't expect this was the answer I would get. But it makes sense now.

In the dream, Tinker Bell said, "...he'll never have his Darling back."

"She killed the original Darling," I say.

Peter exhales beside me.

"So you killed her."

"I wasn't thinking straight," he admits. "Sometimes I

act before I think. Once Tink and the original Darling were dead, it made it much harder to track down my shadow. But memories can be inherited in blood and the original Darling had a little sister. It was improbable, but I'd hoped that any sort of knowledge might have been passed down through her lineage."

The little girl in the closet. She must have been the sister.

"So that's why you take us, trying to find any shred of information about your shadow."

He nods.

"I think I know where it is."

He looks over at me, his hair mussed with sleep, but his eyes wide with anticipation. "Tell me."

"In my great-grandmother Wendy's trunk."

29

PETER PAN

ONE MORE TRIP TO HER WORLD. I CAN MAKE IT.

I have to.

The wait for sunset feels like an eternity. I sent the Darling away so I could pace the room alone.

There is a desperate sense of urgency making my head pound.

While I wait for the sun to set, I strap on as many blades as I can.

When the light finally fades, I race up the stairwell.

Everyone is ready.

"You're all coming?" I ask.

"Of course we are," Bash answers. "You think we'll leave you to have all of the adventures?"

The Darling is set between the twins and looks like a tiny doll against their tallness. Everything about her appears fragile and breakable, but she's anything but.

She reminds me a lot of her mother.

"So how do you get there?" Darling asks.

"Best way is to fly," I answer.

She just stares at me for several long seconds. Then, "Can you fly?"

"Not anymore," I admit.

"And we lost our wings," Kas says.

"Vane?" she asks.

"I can fly, but I'm not hauling all your asses."

"We'll take the other route," I say.

"And what's that?" she asks.

"We leap off Marooner's Rock."

"You must be joking." She sets her hands on her hips. "Please tell me you're joking?"

The twins start off. "We never joke about jumping off cliffs."

"I don't want to jump off a cliff."

"Too bad," I tell her and steer her out the door.

As we make our way through the forest, wolves howl in the distance and we hear one growl from the darkness.

We keep Darling between us, keeping her safe.

The wolves used to bend to me, but not anymore.

We pass the lagoon and keep walking where the land ascends up the cliff's backside.

The moon hangs heavy in the sky.

I thought tonight we'd be inviting Tilly back to dig inside the Darling's head.

I'm glad that we're not. I'm glad the Darling is all right.

Dew has collected on the moss that grows between crevices. It's a cold night and Darling shivers.

Diving into the ocean won't help that, and neither will crossing worlds.

We toe the edge of the cliff as the ocean wind cuts in. Darling's hair billows around her.

"This is much higher than it looks from down below." Her arms are tight over her midsection and she hasn't gotten closer than ten feet from the edge. "I don't think I can do this. Is this how you brought me here?"

"Yes."

She chews at her bottom lip.

"Just think, when we get there, you can stay. You never have to come back here."

Her face falls and my gut clenches.

Is that what I want?

Is that what she wants?

I barely know her and yet she feels familiar.

And the thought of forgetting her once she's gone...

My chest burns.

"Come." I offer her my hand. At the very least, I can promise to be by her side. She slips her hand into mine. Her fingers are ice cold.

"So we just jump?"

"Yes." I urge her closer to the edge.

"Are there rocks down there?"

"Yes, but that's why we'll take a big leap."

"And then what?" She frowns up at me, worry lines furrowing between her brows. "Do we swim? Do we dive?"

"The magic will take care of it for us."

She snorts.

"You just have to believe," Kas says and then he jumps.

"Oh my god," she says on a hiccupping breath. "I can't."

"You must."

"Why?"

Bash jumps next. The wind switches directions and a

lock of hair shoots across Darling's face. I bend down to tuck it behind her ear. "I've got you. All right?"

I swear I can hear her heart pounding over the pounding of the waves.

"All right. Fine."

"Good girl."

I take us toward the edge. Her grip is tight on mine the closer we get.

"Ready?"

"I guess."

"One."

She trembles beside me.

"Two."

Her chest rises and falls with quick breaths.

I don't get to three before we're leaping off the edge together.

This is the only way I can fly these days and it's fucking exhilarating.

But if the Darling is right, by this time tomorrow, I will be flying amongst the stars.

30

WINNIE

WHEN I COME UP FOR AIR, I'M SCREAMING.

There are no waves. No wind. But we're in water. This water is shallow and brackish and it takes me a second to recognize it as Emerald Pond in the park down the street from our old Victorian.

I'm home.

I'm home.

So why am I dreading it?

We trudge out of the water, me and Peter Pan and the Lost Boys.

It's dark here too and crickets and pond frogs chirp and croak in the night.

"This way," I say and move us to the sidewalk that'll take us to the street.

We're all silent as we walk, soaking wet and on a mission. It takes us less than ten minutes to reach the Victorian. Somehow seeing my house with Pan and the boys makes one or both of them feel unreal.

Like they shouldn't exist in the same space.

We go up the cracked and crumbling front walk. I try the door and find it unlocked. That's unlike my mother. She always remembers to lock the doors.

When I push the door in, it creaks on its hinges. The house is dark and quiet save for its normal settling, like old bones creaking.

"Mom?" I call out.

There's no answer.

We go down the hallway and the boys stay behind me.

My great grandmother's trunk is in the living room beneath the bay window.

Except when we reach the doorway, we find Mom there with a man shorter than me, and several more just like him. He's got a shock of dark hair on his head and big, wide-set eyes with pointed ears.

"Brownie," Pan says on a growl.

"Pan," the little man says.

"Why are you here?" Pan asks. There is a very clear edge of suspicion in his voice.

The Brownie steps forward. "Tink didn't want you to be king and I dedicated my life to her."

"But how did you know it was here?" Pan takes another step.

Vane and the twins match his movements, flanking Pan.

"I always knew it was here," the Brownie answers. "To be fair, I thought you'd be dead by now. We all did."

The others nod. There are seven of them in total.

"What do you plan to do with my shadow once you claim it? Not many can hold it."

"The twins could," the Brownie says.

Pan goes rigid. "What's Tilly have to say about that?"

"She wants what's best for the island." The Brownie

rests his hand on the hilt of a blade strapped at his hip. "You were a vicious king. You can't think we want you to return to that?"

I watch Pan's face for a reaction. I know he can be vicious. I watched him kill that Lost Boy for nothing more than flirting with me. But just how vicious is he?

I'm not afraid of him, but maybe I should be.

Maybe jumping off that cliff was the least brave thing I've done in so many days.

"I won't let you stop me," Pan says.

"I won't let you leave here with your shadow," the Brownie says.

There is a quiet, still moment right before fighting breaks out.

Mom is wedged between the corner and the trunk, her arms wrapped around her knees.

I run to her as swords clash.

"Mom? Are you okay?"

"Winnie? Oh, Winnie!" She unfolds herself and wraps her arms around me. "I'm so glad you're back."

"Are you okay?"

"Yes, I'm fine. I'm fine."

I look over my shoulder to see Vane's hands on either side of a Brownie's head. He twists violently and the Brownie's neck snaps.

My stomach rolls.

"Mom, do you know of a hidden compartment in great-grandmother's chest?"

"No. Why?"

I unlatch it and pop the lid open. It smells like it's from

another century and the paper lining is now brittle and coming off in flakes. We've used it to store old linens and blankets, and one photo album that's only a third full.

Someone screams behind us. I don't think it's the boys.

I yank out the blankets, the sheets, and then run my hand along the trunk's interior. How did the Darling in my dream do it?

I start knocking on the inner walls.

Nothing happens.

"Come on."

I think it was the left side of the trunk in my dream. I rap my knuckles again. Once, twice. Nothing.

Maybe I'm not being forceful enough. The Darling in my dream hit the trunk with more of a thump than a knock.

I try again and—

A drawer pops open.

And nestled inside, aged by decades of waiting, is a box.

31

PETER PAN

I FUCKING HATE BROWNIES.

On the island, they're usually scarce, preferring to slink in the shadows rather than be seen in the light. I suppose I can relate to that.

But this Brownie, the one that has been around as long as I have, who has served the fae court, has been out for my blood since I killed Tink.

And maybe I deserve it.

He's quicker than I am, darting in and around me, making deep cuts in my flesh with the blade of his jeweled dagger.

I have one of my blades poised to gut him.

He will not stand between me and my shadow and ultimately my throne.

The others make quick work of the lesser Brownies until only the one remains.

Blood mists the air. I can taste it on the tip of my tongue.

"You're surrounded, Brownie," Vane says as he and the twins circle. Vane just barely has control of his shadow. I sense it bristling beneath the surface, desperate to come out. "Best relent."

"I won't," the Brownie answers. "My princes," he adds and turns to the twins. "If you're looking for a path back to court, then join me now. The shadow can be yours."

Kas and Bash come to a stop and regard one another. I hear the faint tinkling of bells.

I spoke their language once, but I've forgotten the shape of the words, the chime of the syllables.

If they fucking turn on me now...

Bash slides his blade back into its sheath. "There's something we could never quite figure out, Brownie. Maybe you can fill us in."

The Brownie nods. "Anything at all."

"The Darlings are always changed after our dear sister gets inside their heads. She's always told Pan it's a hazard of the magic. That the more a Darling fights it, the worse it'll be."

"Yes, that's true."

"But Merry didn't fight it. She told us before Tilly came that she would do what she could to help Pan."

In the shadows of the room, Darling looks at her mother with new awareness.

"We made Merry a promise that if she helped us, she would be fine. But she wasn't fine."

Merry hiccups on a sob and Darling clutches her mother's hand to her chest.

"So tell us," Kas says as he takes another step. "Was Tilly helping Pan look for the shadow, or was she keeping it from him? Destroying the Darlings' memories so no one would know where it was?"

I grit my teeth, tighten my hold on my sword waiting for the answer.

"Is that true, Brownie?" I ask.

He sputters, tries to get the twins in front of him again, but as Kas distracts him, Bash gets behind him.

"He killed Tink!"

"Our mother was not a virtuous woman," Bash says. "None of us are."

He darts toward the Brownie. The Brownie dances away.

And I lunge with my blade, sinking it deep into his chest. Blood coats his lips.

On a wet, raspy breath he says, "You are no king. You are a coward."

When the blood has drained from his face and the life from his eyes, I pull the blade out. He drops to the floor with a heavy thunk. We are surrounded by bodies and I am coated in blood.

Barely restrained euphoria pulses through me.

Darling lets go of her mother and steps forward. There's a box in her hands.

My shadow.

I've searched for it for so long that I almost don't want to believe this is real.

"Is that it?" I ask.

She comes closer. The box is etched with fae runes. I swear I can still smell Tink on it. Like autumn leaves and fairy dust.

She was my best friend once.

Until she wasn't.

And I'm gutted all over again remembering how it ended.

When I found out what she'd done, that she'd masterminded stealing my shadow as some form of revenge, I'd gone to her and I'd said, *I don't believe in fairies.*

Her light winked out, her eyes went white, and within seconds she was dead.

Just like that.

I didn't even have to get my hands dirty.

The Brownie was right about one thing—I was a coward.

I wish I would have at least given Tink the chance to fight back.

But I think I was afraid of never forgetting what it felt like to have her blood on my hands.

"Should I open it?" Darling asks, forcing me back to the present.

"Not yet. Not until we get back to Neverland. Bash and Kas, start cleaning this mess up."

Bash sighs dramatically. "We turned down the shot of getting our wings back for you. And you make us clean up Brownie guts?"

"We'll get you your wings back. But first you need to do as I ask."

Bash grumbles, then, "Darling, where do you keep your shovels?"

"Ummm..."

Merry is trembling like a leaf, but she answers, nonetheless. "Shovels. Two shovels. In the shed. I'll take you."

"Very well, Merry," Kas says. "Lead the way."

Vane picks up a Brownie, hoists the dead weight over his shoulder and follows the lot out the back door.

It's just me and the Darling.

"You're home now," I tell her. "Thank you for helping me." I hold out my hand for the box.

She tucks it beneath her arm.

"Darling," I say, not bothering to hide the warning from my voice.

"Take me back with you."

"What?"

"Take me back."

"Why?"

She looks around the carnage and frowns.

"There's more than just the shadow," she says.

"What do you mean?"

"I...I don't know. It's nothing more than a gut instinct. But when Tilly got inside my head..."

"Yes?"

"I think she's plotting something. Against you."

"It would seem so." Like mother like daughter, apparently.

"So maybe I can help. I helped you find your shadow."

My first instinct is to leave her here. Whatever is waiting for me in Neverland, it won't be good.

"You'll be safer here."

Her gaze hardens. "Safer is not what I want."

I have a sudden flash of bending her over the table. Pretty Darling girl wants dark, vile things done to her.

I would be lying if I said I didn't want that too.

I want her wet cunt wrapped around my cock.

The moment I met her, I knew she was different. I don't know what it is about her but it reminds me of something old and forgotten.

"I have rules," I tell her. "Rules that are meant to be followed."

She smiles sweetly up at me and I know already that she'll be trouble if I bring her back.

"I can follow rules."

"Yes, but will you?"

Vane returns and lifts another Brownie onto his shoulder. "Twins have a hole dug already."

I nod. If he thinks I'm burying dead bodies, he's sorely mistaken.

"Bring me back with you," Darling says again.

We've always been a house of cold, hard edges...would it be so bad to have someone with soft curves, someone to share? Fuck her and make her quiver, make her beg for Lost Boy cum.

I am not a nice man and I want to do very bad things to her. And with my shadow, the possibilities are endless.

"Fine," I tell her. "You can come back with me."

She smiles triumphantly up at me.

"Don't get cocky."

"I won't. I'll just get cock."

"Darling girl with a filthy mouth. Now come, let us go supervise the burying of Brownies while the night is still young."

"First," she says and holds out the box. "I think this belongs to you."

In all the years I've been searching for my shadow, I could never feel it. I ached for it, but where it used to be was nothing but a void.

I can sense it now.

The writhing energy of it trapped in that box.

I reach out and take it.

"Thank you."

She smiles. "You're welcome, Peter Pan."

32

WINNIE

THERE'S SOMETHING ABOUT MOM NOW THAT FEELS SETTLED. LIKE if she were a top, all of the spin has gone out of her and she's finally sitting still.

The moonlight shines on the macabre scene in our backyard. There is a giant hole in the center where bodies are starting to pile up.

"Isn't this risky?" I ask. And also...I can't believe I'm in my backyard with two fae princes, a myth, and a shadow of death burying bodies six feet in the ground.

I don't know how or when I became a person that took this all in with no issue.

"Don't worry, Darling," Kas says. "Brownies turn to dust within a week."

As the boys finish up the dirty work, I turn to Mom. "I need to tell you something."

"What is it, baby?" She is paler than when I left her, but her face is clean, as is her hair, so clearly she's been taking care of herself without me to look after her.

"I'm going back," I tell her. "To Neverland."

Her eyes are on me but I'm never entirely sure if she's seeing me.

"Do you want to come with me?"

I didn't run this past Pan, but I don't care. The house has many spare rooms. There's plenty of room for her.

"Come to Neverland?" she asks and looks back at the boys. Bash is shirtless and is shoveling dirt in, all of the corded muscle in his back working overtime.

God, he is a sight. A fae prince who I think might be mine. I can't be sure yet. I don't know what the rules are about all that, but there's plenty of time to figure it out.

One thing I am absolutely sure of is that I will fight anyone who thinks they can take him from me.

I might have only scratched the surface of who Peter Pan and the Lost Boys are, but instinct never lies and they feel like mine.

They *are* mine.

"I don't think I want to," Mom says.

"Really?"

"I...here...listen—"

"I'm listening, Mom."

"I like it here." She glances up at the house painted in broad strokes of moonlight. "I feel better."

"But...you'll be all alone."

"I'll be okay."

I was an adult before I ever had a chance to be a child. And I always looked after my mom. I never wanted to. Her endless episodes, the instability, I hated every part of it.

And while I wanted to escape it, now that I'm faced with the possibility, I'm terrified of doing it.

"Mom—"

"Go." She squeezes my hand. "Go to Neverland. The mermaids will be happy you've returned."

The mermaids? Right, the spirits in the lagoon.

"If you're sure..."

"Yes."

I slide my arm around her shoulders and pull her into me. "I'll come back to check on you as much as I can." As soon as I get over the heart-pounding fear of jumping off a cliff.

She smiles to herself. "I would like that, baby."

When the hole is full and all of the Brownie blood is cleaned from the floor, the boys stand outside looking like visions of war covered in blood and dirt, smoke from several lit cigarettes curling in the moonlight.

"If you need me," I start to say to Mom and then realize there's no way for her to reach me. There are no cell phones on Neverland. No form of communication.

"I'll be okay, Winnie." She hugs me and when she pulls back, she says, "Do you want to know a secret?"

"Yes."

"I wanted to stay too, before they broke my head."

"Really?"

"I miss the magic." She closes her eyes, sinks into the memories. "And the—"

"Cloudberries," I guess.

"Yes."

"I'll bring you some next time."

"And then I'll make pies and cakes and we'll have a party."

"If you'd like."

Her eyes glaze over again.

"Why don't you go make yourself some tea and rest?"

"Okay, baby."

"I love you, Mom."

"I love you too." She slips away from me and shuts the door and I stay there on the front porch for a long time trying to decide if I'm making the right decision.

Will she be okay without me?

She loved me fiercely, but her love always hurt.

I don't know how it feels to be loved the right way or to choose to feel the hurt instead of being forced into it.

Maybe that's what love really is, at the heart of it —*choosing* the pain with the pleasure.

I return to the boys. I can tell by their energy that they're growing impatient, but they weren't prepared to rush me.

"I'm ready," I say.

Peter Pan takes my hand and leads me off into the night, the little box containing his shadow tucked beneath his arm.

EPILOGUE

PETER PAN

WHAT WILL IT FEEL LIKE, HAVING MY SHADOW BACK?

It's been so long that I think I've forgotten how it felt to be full and flush with magic. To be able to create anything out of nothing. To feel the island's beating heart.

I am suddenly desperate for it and terrified of it all at the same time.

We're back in the loft. Vane is at the bar pouring us all drinks. The twins are on the couch with Darling nestled between them.

I have done a great many terrible things in my life and believing that I can be so lucky to have a great many great things now seems naïve.

Vane brings the glasses over. He's chosen an aged whiskey that smells like smokey wood and caramel. I test a sip, relishing the burn.

"We ready for this?" Vane asks as he drops into one of the leather chairs.

"Ready as we'll ever be, I suspect," Bash says.

"What does this even look like?" Darling asks. "Like, does it have shape? Or is it just a puff of smoke?"

"It will look exactly like a shadow should," I admit. "But the real question is, did Tink tether it to something when she put it in the box or will it dart away when we open it?"

"We'll be ready to spring," Vane says. "You have our word."

I take another pull from the glass and set it on the table between us, right next to the little box. There is a single latch on it, no lock.

My heart is beating so hard in my chest, I can feel it in my teeth.

We all take a collective breath as I reach forward and undo the latch, putting my fingers to the lid.

We're all leaning forward now, the anticipation, the excitement a palpable thing.

This is it, this is what I've been waiting for.

I push open the lid...

...and two shadows leap out.

I hope you enjoyed this dark, twisted version of Neverland and the characters who inhabit it. I loved writing Winnie Darling. She's fierce and blunt and she's not afraid to go after what she wants.

If you want to return to Neverland with Winnie, be sure to pre-order book two, The Dark One, so you don't miss out!

WANT TO JOIN OTHER NEVER KING READERS TO DISCUSS ALL THINGS WINNIE & PAN & THE LOST BOYS?

Come join the reader group Nikki St. Crowe's Nest on Facebook!
https://www.facebook.com/groups/nikkistcrowesnest/

ALSO BY NIKKI ST. CROWE

VICIOUS LOST BOYS

The Never King

The Dark One

WRATH & RAIN TRILOGY

Ruthless Demon King

Sinful Demon King

Vengeful Demon King

HOUSE ROMAN

A Dark Vampire Curse

MIDNIGHT HARBOR

Hot Vampire Next Door (ongoing Vella serial)

Hot Vampire Next Door: Season One (ebook)

Hot Vampire Next Door: Season Two (ebook)

Hot Vampire Next Door: Season Three (ebook)

Vampire's Good Girl: A Hot Vampire Prequel (ongoing Vella serial)

ABOUT THE AUTHOR

NIKKI ST. CROWE has been writing for as long as she can remember. Her first book, written in the 4th grade, was about a magical mansion full of treasure. While she still loves writing about magic, she's ditched the treasure for something better: villains, monsters, and anti-heroes, and the women who make them wild.

These days, when Nikki isn't writing or daydreaming about villains, she can either be found on the beach or at home with her husband and daughter.

NIKKI'S NEWSLETTER: https://www.
subscribepage.com/nikkistcrowe

GAIN EARLY ACCESS TO COVER REVEALS AND SNEAK PEEKS ON
PATREON: https://www.patreon.com/nikkistcrowe

JOIN NIKKI'S READER GROUP:
https://www.facebook.com/groups/nikkistcrowesnest/

VISIT NIKKI ON THE WEB AT:
www.nikkistcrowe.com

CPSIA information can be obtained
at www.ICGtesting.com
Printed in the USA
LVHW051828270423
745407LV00004B/276